CW00382081

PRICE MANOR: THE HOUSE THAT FALLS

The House That Falls: Book Three in the *Price Manor* series from Deadline Horror Collective. A horror novella.

First edition published 2022 by Jay Alexander in association with Deadline Horror Collective. Thank you for buying an authorised copy of this book.

TRADE PAPERBACK ISBN: 9798436053868

PRICE MANOR
BOOK THREE

THE HOUSE THAT FALLS

A NOVELLA BY

JAY ALEXANDER

CHAPTER ONE
THE BUTCHER'S TABLE (I)

When Charlie finally returned from the dead, stomach bleeding into his hands, he was strapped down on a cool, marble worktop. Knives hung from the ceiling, glinting in a strange, pink light that came from outside. With a great effort, he turned his head toward the window; the panes were smeared with blood.

But that was after.

CHAPTER TWO
BEFORE

The battlefield at the foot of the hill had spread and ruptured outwards, up and over the grassy mound of earth, so that now the hill itself was no more than a blistered lump of smouldering chaos: rivers of red and grey streaked the banks, blood and gun-smoke rolling down from the crest like the violent spittle of an emptied volcano. Bodies littered the ground.

The air was dry and mild. In the December of 1648, the Thames had frozen; January had brought rain, and even now, at the beginning of spring, it looked as though the onslaught of the sky would last for as long as the war did. The battle had been blessed, however, by respite; the rain had stopped, and the field had been almost dry when they had fought.

Now they were all dead and the ground was wet again, dirt soaked with blood and ichor. There was mist, despite the brittle quality of the air; thick, grey mist that stunk of gunpowder. In it, a handful of figures rolled and twitched. The near-dead; defeated, but left to cling to their defeat.

Halfway up the hill, the eyes of a scrawny, black-haired carcass snapped wide open. Morgan's helmet—a bulky, rusted clamp of metal that always seemed too tight for his skull—had rolled off, and his face was spattered with soot, hair matted and pressed to his scalp. He breathed harshly, sucking in the air. His lungs had been wrecked by the blood he'd inhaled; he drew in a gasp of powdery mist and coughed again. Warmth spread through his mouth. Blinking rapidly, he rolled onto his side, clutching at his ribs. With one hand he scrambled for his rifle; it was nowhere to be found. 'No,' he murmured, crawling forward. His left leg burned; something had torn the back of his calf open. All around, he smelled death. It smelled like half-groat pieces. The new ones, with the cross of St. George having replaced the king's head (shame, he thought, that nobody had considered jamming a cross into the bloody stump of the flesh-and-blood king's neck when his own head had been lopped off), smelled particularly crisp; that was what this was like. Metal drifted on the air. 'Come on,' Morgan whispered, clawing at the ground for his musket, 'got to be round here somewhere...'

His fingers found something soft and fleshy. He drew back, patted the ground around what he presumed was an exposed shoulder or kneecap. Straining to see through bunches of grey smoke that coiled around him, he scratched at the grass, swiping forward.

'Ah!' he hissed, his knuckles knocking something hard. He dragged his fingers along the shaft of the thing; polished wood, worn down in places with use. He grinned. Reached out with both hands to grab the rifle, and pulled. Something tugged back. He paused. Pulled at it again. there was a wet *crunch*. The mist rolled back.

The wide eyes of a pale, grey face stared into his own. The tongue of the fallen soldier lolled out of its mouth and poked at the ground; a slug had started to crawl up it and into the dead man's mouth. Morgan screamed. Looked down. Gloved hands gripped the stock of the rifle. The musket was marred with blood.

'Looking for this?' came a voice from behind him.

Morgan rolled onto his back, grunting as something scraped the wound at the back of his leg. 'I'm not—don't shoot—' he started.

A silhouette stepped out of the mist. He picked out narrow eyes, a flash of pink skin. The man wore the bunchy, blue-and-red uniform of a Roundhead. Morgan's chest flooded with relief and he lowered his hands. 'Not many left round here, huh?' said the silhouette.

Morgan shook his head. 'We... we were slaughtered. There were too many. We drove some back, into the woods, I think'—his throat erupted with a bloody series of coughs—'they'll be... back.'

The silhouette took another step forward. Smoke rolled across his legs and chest. He was old, forty-five or fifty, perhaps, his brow and cheeks weathered with lines. A thick, orange beard clung to his chin, the glorious curls of a moustache almost brushing his ears. He held out a rifle. 'How many went into the woods?'

Morgan dragged himself to his rump, breathing hard. 'I don't know. Ten, twenty. Plus any that survived the battle, I suppose.'

The silhouette with the red beard nodded. 'Makes sense. Here.'

Morgan grabbed the barrel of the gun and hauled himself to his feet. The older man grunted as he passed the rifle over. He had another slung over his shoulder, the leather band pressing into his chest. There was a pin on his left breast, Morgan saw, a ceramic emblem that he didn't recognise. 'What's—'

'Me? Abram, son. General Oliver Abram. And yourself?'

'Morgan,' the young man said. He lowered the rifle, jabbed the wide barrel into the soil so that he could lean on it and take the weight off his bad leg. With his free hand, he pointed to the badge. 'I mean, what's that?'

The badge was about the size of a coin—again, Morgan was reminded of the smell of blood all around them—and etched into the shape of a tilted cross—an X, he supposed—laid over a grinning skull. 'Ah, I see,' Abram said, and his mouth tilted into a thin smile of its own. 'General Oliver Abram of the *Nowhere Boys*.' He tapped the badge. 'You haven't heard of us?'

Morgan shook his head. He heard footsteps across the ridge.

'Well, whaddya know,' Abram said, 'I guess it all worked out, then, son.'

'We've got another one!' a voice yelled from somewhere in the mist. A female voice.

'He looks bad!' came another. Male, gruff. Morgan heard the owner of the second voice murmur something, but couldn't make out the words.

'Sounds like you weren't the only lucky one,' Abram said, clapping a hand on the young man's shoulder. 'Come on, son. Let me introduce you to the rest of the Boys.'

Morgan nodded.

Abram hesitated. 'Oh, and... watch the bodies while you walk. Don't want to step on any of your friends.'

CHAPTER THREE
THE NOWHERE BOYS

Edith led Michael through the smoking ruins of the field, swinging her pike in slow, deliberate arcs. The badge on her chest glinted as thin curls of sunlight tried to break through the smog above. 'Christ Jesus,' she whispered, thick traces of an Irish accent peeling out of her lips, 'I didn't think we had parties out this deep in Royalist country. No wonder they were massacred.'

Behind her, Michael grunted. 'We're out here, ain't we?'

'We're different,' she said, turning her head. 'You all right there, Shuck? You look a little pale.'

Michael Caldwell glared at her. Dark, rough-cut hair framed a stern face, three long, white scars—scars that looked like the claw-marks of some demon dog—brushed his right cheek. 'Enough with the nicknames, *Missy*. Let's just get this over with so we can move on from this little detour.'

Edith cocked an eyebrow. A narrow face, smeared with sweat and grit, pinched itself in disregard. 'You really that desperate to finish our mission?'

Michael said nothing.

Edith shrugged and kept walking, stepping over outstretched arms and legs. Blood had splashed her boots; her toes were as red as the trousers of her uniform. Her helmet had long been discarded—as had those of the others; there was no use in covering their skulls, not when the unarmoured fabric of their garments left the rest of their bodies so exposed—and her hair was pinned back into a bun that had exploded across the back of her neck.

All around them, the dead rose and fell with the mist. It was like walking along the beach, she thought, with the thin, grey waves rolling back and forth and bringing the bobbing, half-swimming bodies of the drowned with them. Sagging chests, smashed in by shot and pooling with red, were still. Torn throats steamed in the cold, thin rivulets running off the bloody chins and faces of Roundheads and Cavaliers alike.

'They're all dead,' Michael said, shaking his head as he swung his gun over his shoulder. 'Let's find the boss and get out of here.'

Edith stood among the carcasses for a moment and glanced around. They were all so young. Some of them could hardly have been out of their teens, while those that were had only just left those formative years behind; these were lives snuffed out too soon, lives lost to blood and carnage for the latter's sake. King Charles was dead, and with the *thud* of his empty head on the ground so too had died many of the Cavaliers' dreams—yet, they still fought like animals. Stinking, bastard animals killing not because it furthered their cause but because they'd grown to love it; killing for sport. And the poor Roundheads scattered around her... what were they fighting for, now? To survive? To *win*? There was no winning; even with the death of the king, this country was lost. Cromwell had all but won, but at what cost?

'Yeah,' she said quietly. 'Let's.'

And then something moved.

'Wait...'

Michael shook his head. 'What?'

Raising a finger, Edith hushed him. 'Wait...'

There. Again. Something *twitched*, half-buried in a pile of burgundy-clothed corpses to her left. She pointed.

'There.'

Michael moved for the pile-up, bent down on one knee to dig through the carcasses. His thumb plunged into a wet eye-socket, Edith noticed, but he didn't seem to care. She hadn't known him long, but she knew that he'd grown up rough; way out in the sticks, hunting and farming for food, keeping his family alive and getting bloody doing it. He had plumbed his digits into the bloody bowls of enough skulls, she supposed.

'Found him?'

'Yeah,' Michael grunted, hauling a body out of the wreckage. A kid, Edith saw, barely *in* his teens—let alone on his way out of them.

His flesh was pale, his eyes closed. His helmet crashed against his skull as he was pulled free. Curls of brown poked out from beneath the rim. His ribs were caved in, his right arm broken. His blue jacket had been torn and the damp mess of an undershirt showed through, spotted with red. 'Breathing,' Michael said, 'but only just.'

He laid the kid down, and Edith watched as a spasm rocked his little body. 'Poor bastard,' she said quietly. Cupping a hand around her mouth, she yelled into the mist: 'We've got another one!'

'He looks bad!' Michael called out. Shooting Edith a look, he said, 'We ought to put him down while he's asleep. Look at this shit.' He pointed to the kid's stomach. A deep, red pool lay across the fabric of his uniform, swilling left and right as violent twitches tore at his ragged figure.

'Don't be such a dog,' Edith hissed. 'Unless you want that nickname to stick.'

'Fuck you.'

Abram called to them through the smog, then: 'Does he look like a fighter?'

They looked upon the body. Christ, the kid could only have been fifteen, sixteen at best. The right side of his face was scratched and bruised—Edith saw Michael surveying the damage to his cheek and wondered if he was reminiscing over his own injuries—and his knuckles were raw. He had no rifle. No belt. His boots were scuffed from kicking.

'Half dead,' she called back, 'but if we can get him on his feet—'

'—big *if*,' Michael said.

'*If* we can, then,' she hissed, then turned to yell again: 'He'll be fine!'

Two figures appeared from within the smoke. Abram had picked up some young, dark-haired lad from the ground, and the thin man held a rifle that had seen better days; the stock was worn and scratched, the barrel blossoming with rust. 'Edith, Michael,' Abram nodded, 'meet Morgan. He'll be coming with us.'

The newcomer shook his head. 'I won't get in the way,' he said. 'I can go back—'

'None of that,' Edith said. She cast a questioning look in Abram's direction; he nodded. 'You're one of us, now. We've lost enough of our team. If we can fix you up, can you help?'

'Help with what?' Morgan said, his eyes appealing. He looked exhausted. Battered. His left leg sagged.

'Nothing,' Michael murmured.

'Well, for starters, you can help us lift this youngun away from here,' Abram nodded at the ground. 'Any idea who he is?'

Morgan looked at the boy for a long moment. 'Not a clue,' he said. He frowned. 'I don't recognise him.'

Edith shrugged. 'Did you know many of them?'

'Not by name, I suppose,' Morgan said. 'It's just... he looks so young. It's sad.'

Michael knelt by the twitching body, pressing two fingers to his exposed throat. 'He's fading. We need to get him inside fast.'

'Inside?' Morgan said, his face blank.

Abram frowned at him. 'The house over the ridge,' he said. 'About a quarter-mile from here. Thought we'd set up camp there a little while, just an hour or so, get you boys healed up—then we'll head on. We've got things to do.'

Morgan shook his head. 'The woods—'

'I know,' the older man said. 'There're Cavaliers in the woods. Twenty or so, you say? Thirty, perhaps, depending how many walked away from... *this*. But we'll be safe there for a short time. Barricade the door, move out when we're able.'

'No, you don't understand,' Morgan said, almost desperately. 'We scoured this whole area. I *know* the fields around here. The woods... the woods are *all there is for miles*.'

'The fuck is he trying to say?' Michael said.

'I'm saying there *is* no house around here,' Morgan said. 'There's nothing.'

Edith and Morgan carried the body of the boy over the hill. Michael Caldwell had gone on ahead to scout the short distance between the battlefield and the house, and General Oliver Abram followed behind. He hadn't said anything since Morgan had claimed the fields here were empty; he seemed lost in thought.

The boy coughed, once, in their arms, but didn't awaken. Michael had dug inside his clothes and found a slip of identification marking him as *Charles Buxton*; Morgan had seen the boy's stomach, almost completely open and spewing a steady flow of blood, and balked.

The dead watched them move, wide eyes staring unblinking at the sky. Abram grabbed knives and shells as they came down the far slope of the hill, stuffing them into an empty Cavalier hat—the feathered plume painted red with blood—that he was using as a bowl.

Morgan was walking backwards, his hands dug into the boy's armpits, so he didn't see the house until it was looming over them. As the sky darkened, the shadow of the building falling over them, he turned his head to look. His mouth dropped open. 'What...'

'So you're telling me this shit wasn't here before?' Michael sneered from the front door.

'I...'

'Extreme stress,' Abram explained drily. 'We've all been there.'

'No, I—it—'

He caught Edith's eye. She was looking thoughtfully at him. She shook her head subtly. Probably for the best, Morgan thought. Figure out how it got here later. For now...

They set the body down and he stepped back, looked up at the house. Three stories tall, it was a Gothic pillar of black brick and moulded stone: the roof was buttressed, black shingles rolling in cascades to a great point that prodded madly at the falling sun, each prick deflating it so that it had begun to sunk; the windows were narrow and dark, some of the panes splintered. The door was massive and framed by a great stone arch; support structures held and brickwork beams held the rest on their arms, although it looked too heavy even for the gods that kept the sky up. It looked dark, foreboding... *forbidding*.

'Door's open,' Michael said. 'All ours.'

That sent a shiver down Morgan's spine. His mouth opened. Closed again. He looked up—up, up, all the way to the top...

Something moved in an upstairs window. He blinked. It was gone.

Edith nudged him in the ribs. 'You coming?'

Her smile dragged him back to earth and he nodded, bending down to slip his arms under the limp shoulders of the half-dead kid. They turned, carried him toward the door; Abram had already gone inside. Michael was waiting, holding it open.

Morgan looked up again as a cold pain drifted up his neck.

A tall, thin man stood in the frame of a window at the very top of the house, looking down at them. Morgan caught the flash of teeth; said, 'Hey, there's someone—'

And then the man was gone. He paused.

'Where?' Edith said, tipping her head right back to follow his gaze.

Morgan shook his head. 'Must have imagined it,' he said.

'Must've,' Michael grunted, ushering them in.

Morgan swallowed, shuddered off the cool, damp feeling, and pressed through the front door of the house that wasn't there.

CHAPTER FOUR
CAME TO BE

Oliver Abram had only screamed once in his life: the day he was born. He wasn't sure exactly what day that might have been; his mother, a red-haired woman named Elizabeth Becker (she and his father had never married—they might have done, if things had gone differently), and his father, Thomas Abram, had never been the type of people to celebrate the passing of time. And what with his being only three years old when they died—Elizabeth trampled by horses, and Thomas, two days later, at the barrel of the musket in his own hands—all he knew was that it must have been somewhere between the spring of 1600 and the winter of 1601.

Since then, he had wept twice: once, that he could recall, at the birth of his daughter, and once at her death (typhoid). He had shed the odd tear here or there, and had choked up when, in July 1644, eight of his men had perished at the battle of Marston Moor. He had accepted his fate with a grim stolidity when Cromwell had assigned him, secretly, as the leader of the Nowhere Boys; he had mourned silently when this blackmarked band's numbers dwindled from ten to eight, to seven, six, and then to three.

Not since the day he was born—and even then, he only *imagined* he had wailed like any other child—had he ever *screamed*.

That would change.

When Oliver Abram came into the world, screaming, at the hazy beginning of the seventeenth century, there was no house in the field six miles east of Sorrow Helm—a field that was known, then, as Sorrow's Hollow.

*

Edith was born some time later, but her birth

was uninteresting, her family unremarkable. She always thought that her life had only truly begun when she'd run away from them; not because they were wicked, or cruel, or even because her childhood had been so unnotably boring, but for a boy. His name was Edmund, and she'd imagined they were meant for each other. He was older, but that didn't matter. He was kind, and his eyes were like sharp little gems that she sliced her open whenever she looked into them.

She had left home with him, *for* him, made her whole life about him—and on their first night together, she had almost expected to become one with him. But Edmund had kissed her cheek in the bedroom of the dingy inn they'd booked for the night, said he needed to walk, to clear his head, and left.

He hadn't come back.

When she came down to the empty inn the next morning, she discovered he'd stayed up till long after midnight drinking, then left at around half-past two in the morning. She wondered about between. Giggling, the young, dark-haired barmaid told her: he had followed her down to the wine cellar and made love to her between the kegs.

At precisely the moment Edith's heart broke for good, the field six miles east of Sorrow Helm was empty—save for a dormouse, which moments later would be scooped up by a tawny owl and ripped to shreds.

At the moment Edith shoved the young barmaid into a wooden shelf and split open her skull, the field was still empty. Just a rolling, lumpen plane of grass stained brown by the sun.

As she backed away, horrified, hand over her mouth, gaping at the still body in a pool of candlelit blood before her, a tiny scrap of dormouse intestine dropped into the grass; the owl fluttered away.

Still no house.

A young Charles Buxton saw a recruitment poster—crude, handwritten—pinned to the front door of the ironsmith's three doors down from his parents' home at exactly 10:46

on August 7th, 1647. He was thirteen at the time.

By now, the field had been renamed: Sorrow's Hollow was now known by the locals—sparse as they were—as the Devil's Backyard. Apparently, someone had seen Him playing there.

But it was still empty.

Michael Caldwell never ran away from home, but he'd considered it many times. He was the runt of the litter—even before he earned his nickname, he was doggish and scrappy—and although his father picked on him the least, he still earned his share of cuts and bruises. By the time he was ten years old, his ribs were black with welts and his heart had nearly given out a good dozen times. The scars on his face were not there—not yet—but he had watched his father beat his sister Eleanor to death, and the scars that had been left by that would be there for the rest of his life.

Michael's father died when he was twenty-three, four years before Charles Buxton—

Charlie, to his friends—signed up to join the armed forces amassing in the countryside. The cause was strangulation. The constable called to the house did not pursue the case further; but this was only fair, since he was the owner of the recently-opened post office on Giles Lane and this extracurricular role as law enforcer was an unpaid one. Perhaps Michael's father's killer had known this would be the way of things. Perhaps not.

Either way, if one were to have walked across the fields surrounding Sorrow Helm at around the time the constable had entered the Caldwell family's kitchen to find Mr. Caldwell himself slumped over the table, his neck pink and purple, one would have found nothing but grass and the embers of grass for miles around, making up one wide stretch of pale green hemmed in on all sides by the forest.

No house. Nothing.

*

Six hours before the Nowhere Boys found

Morgan Fossey's half-broken body on the banks of the hill, he and twenty-three men had scouted the site thoroughly, rifles trained on the tree line, eyes scouring the ground. The top of the hill seemed a good place to make camp for the night; good visibility all around, and were they to be ambushed from within the forest they'd have the high ground.

Of course, less than twenty minutes after they'd established a pair of canvas tents at the top of the hill and a small fire, they would be attacked by a force of forty-odd Cavaliers—but that didn't matter. No, what mattered was that Morgan had *checked* these fields. Had made an inventory of everything they'd found between the horseshoe curls of forest at either side of the hill; nothing. Zero. A couple of animal carcasses, and a wide swathe of grass.

There was no house here.

And yet, now it stood, three storeys of black amid the rolling smoke of war: Price Manor, the house that shouldn't have been but had come to be. As if it had simply popped into existence amid all the dying and shrieking and the roar of firing muskets.

Perhaps that was exactly what had happened.

CHAPTER FIVE
THE KITCHEN

Stepping into the house was like waking from a dream: outside, everything had been blue and hazy, roiling and bathing in the smouldering ashes of something half-remembered; walking over the threshold, Michael Caldwell felt that he was finally walking on solid ground.

'Christ,' Edith said behind him. He barely heard her. He stood in the middle of a grand hallway, gazing up at an arched ceiling that looked thirty or thirty-five feet high, his arms hanging by his sides. His rifle was in his left hand; he didn't remember removing it from the leather sling over his shoulder.

He wanted to be unimpressed by the architecture of the entrance hall, but there was something real and hungry about it, something bright and blistering; the walls were a faded, velvety grey and although the paper was peeling in places the designs etched into it were still fresh; golden antlers were pressed to the wall, thousands upon thousands of them, interlocking and weaving together so that they almost formed a map of tines and curved points. A maze of golden spines bending and coiling together, all around. The floorboards were long and narrow, ancient pine varnished smooth; a blood-red rug was laid at the far end of the hall, and atop it stood a tall, glass-fronted cabinet. An elaborate set of wooden stairs wound up to what must have been an upper floor, but the shadows were so deep at the ceiling that it looked as if they simply slipped away into the dark. Gilded rose-heads wound around the banister. He frowned; vines had been carved into the wood, thorns and all, so that anyone walking up would have to move without gripping it, or risk jabbing their flesh on deliberately pointed splinters.

'In here,' Abram commanded. Michael turned, noting three closed doors; two behind him, and one by the staircase. An open doorway near the entrance of the house seemed to lead into a kitchen; this was the room Abram had gestured toward. Edith nodded, and she and the wounded Roundhead carried his fallen comrade gently through the door.

Michael hesitated. There was something about the kitchen...

After a moment, Abram walked up to him. His boots clicked loudly on the wooden floor. 'Everything all right, Caldwell?' he asked quietly.

Michael nodded, keeping his eyes on the open doorway; through it, he could only see shades of blue and pink, but there was something *about* those shades of blue and pink, something unnatural, like they didn't belong together...

'Caldwell?'

And the way the light hit the walls in that room, the way the shadows from the doorway crept forth and lingered on the tiles—

'Are you listening to me, Shuck?'

Michael turned. 'Everything's *fine*, boss,' he

seethed.

Abram nodded curtly. He looked up. Looked around. His hands were gathered behind his back, pinning the musket to his spine. 'Odd place, all the way out here,' he murmured. 'Long abandoned, I should think. No furniture.'

Michael frowned, turning to glance toward the cabinet he'd seen against the far wall.

There was nothing there.

'Yeah...' he said. 'Odd.'

Abram shrugged. 'Still, it'll do for a couple of hours.' He turned to follow the others into the kitchen.

Michael grabbed his arm, gripped it tightly. 'A couple of hours, sir?' he said through gritted teeth. 'You said an hour. We can't hang around—'

Abram yanked at his arm, a flash of annoyance darting across his face. 'We've two wounded men out there, Caldwell—'

'—not *our* men—'

'—all those serving under Cromwell are *our* men, Caldwell.'

Michael cocked an eyebrow. 'Our mission—

'

'Our mission can wait, *Shuck*. Get your hand off me.'

Michael released his grip and took a step back. 'We need to move on,' he said coldly.

'We will. And the sooner you get in here and help me fix up these men, the sooner we move.'

Michael shook his head stiffly.

'At ease, soldier,' Abram said softly. 'We're nearly there.'

'Hm.'

'See you in there.' Abram turned away, disappeared into the kitchen.

For a long moment, Michael stood in the hall, skin tightening as a dreadful cold settled across him. The house seemed to be watching... no, waiting. After a while, he turned. Looked toward the very back of the entrance hall.

The glass-fronted cabinet stood in the shadows, the transparent panes of two narrow doors glinting in the half-light coming from... somewhere. His eyes flitted up; he saw it, hanging from the shadowy pit of the ceiling: a black-pronged chandelier, the candles all lit. They hadn't been before; he would have seen.

Slowly, he moved toward the cabinet at the back of the hall. He gripped the rifle tight. He had crudely attached a serrated blade to the barrel and now he unscrewed it as he walked, never taking his eyes off the cabinet. The knife came free with a sound like stone scraping stone; he fixed the rifle to his back and brandished the blade as he neared the cabinet...

He knelt before it. Peered in through the glass. His reflection was hazy and red on the smooth surface of the door; the scars on his cheek shone.

Empty.

'Huh,' he said, turning back and standing straight. He cracked his neck, gently massaging the muscles of his shoulder, and headed for the kitchen.

*

Charlie lay convulsing on the kitchen table, a

polished, white-topped affair that looked wholly out of place—too large for the room, too small for the young man's body that thrashed and bucked upon it.

The air changed.

'Here, help,' Edith said, looking up to see Michael standing in the doorway. She beckoned him over. She was pinning down the boy's legs, but his left knee jerked wildly and she couldn't reach it across the table. A series of loud knocks echoed about the room as the legs of the table scraped the tiles; pink and blue, scattered around randomly in varying shades so that one was immediately disoriented upon looking down at the floor.

Michael moved to the table across from her and gripped Charlie's leg, pressing it down with such force that Edith was almost surprised there wasn't an audible *crack*.

Morgan looked across the table at the newcomer. He was holding down Charlie's left shoulder, one hand pressed to the boy's ribs; Abram held down Charlie's head. Blood flowed from his stomach onto the table and drizzled over the clean, white edges onto the floor. 'I don't know what's wrong with him,' Morgan said.

'You think I do?' Michael said, looking around as the boy's knee jerked beneath his palm. Anxiety filled the room.

Edith shook her head. 'We need laudanum, at least. To stop... this.' Charlie kicked blindly at her; he was breathing hard, now, his chest rising and falling, pumping blood from his open gut with every inhalation. Squeezing it from him. He moaned as he slept.

'He's suffering,' Michael said coolly. 'We should have left him out there. We should finish him now.'

'We need him,' Abram said. There was something hard and stiff about the way he spoke.

Edith swallowed. 'Right,' she nodded in Michael's direction. 'Get his legs. I'm going to see if there's anything we can use in the pantry.'

'Bandages, too,' Abram said. 'For his stomach.'

'You don't have any of this stuff?' Morgan said, 'in a pack, or something?'

Michael snarled. 'We *did*,' he said, scowling in Abram' direction.

Abram threw an apologetic look back at him, but said nothing.

Edith nodded, backing up. She turned, glancing briefly out through the window above a clean, metal basin. Outside, she saw nothing but grey and the dark, smudged silhouettes of the trees in the distance. No time, she thought. No time...

The worktops were granite, the edges crushed and sharp. A metal block in one corner gripped half a dozen knives by their blades; cupboards all around the room were shut, white-panelled doors held fast. The tiled walls were the same blue-pink kaleidoscope as the floor; everything looked... too clean, too *new*... wholly out of time. She shuddered and crossed the room.

The pantry door was closed, pinned to the frame by a thin, black latch. Above the door, a narrow sign was etched with the words *Food Store*, but the legend was flat and blunt, not scripted in cursive as she was used to.

This was how she imagined a house a

hundred years—two, three-hundred—in the future might look.

Quickly, she opened the door. She had already scanned the cupboards and found little of use: cutlery, utensils, cans of beans and dried food; this was their last chance.

The room was dark. 'Shite,' she whispered, turning back. 'Matches?'

Abram shook his head. She looked in Michael's direction; he looked grimly back at her.

'I have some,' Morgan said. Dark hair fell in his face as he scrambled inside his uniform and produced a slim tin box of sulphur matches. He tossed it to her. She caught it deftly and nodded her thanks, turning back to the pantry. She stepped forward, lighting a match on the second strike, and raised it high—

'What the—' she started, and then the door closed behind her. A gust carried past her and the match flame disappeared, leaving her blinking in the dark. Purple spots danced before her eyes and she swore again, clawing for another match.

FKKASH

The flame leapt up and she looked around. 'Jesus, what the hell...'

In the dim, flickering light, she saw pink-and-blue tiled walls, pristine countertops; no, not pristine, but coated in a thin, murky layer of dust. But the table was there, in the centre of the room, and the window above the sink—although boarded up—was in the same place: she had left one kitchen and entered another. Two adjoining rooms that looked almost identical, except this one had clearly been abandoned months before the first. A spider's web in one corner twitched nervously as something squirmed within it; a crack along the far wall—

The match burnt out and she yelped as heat blistered her thumb. 'God fuck it,' she hissed, striking another.

FKKASH

The crack was shallow and black; ants crawled from it where it met the skirting board.

'Weird,' she murmured, sidestepping the table as she crossed the room to another door, this one also marked *Food Store*. The match shrivelled as she opened it; stepping through, she went to strike another...

And stopped. The room was lit. Light streamed in through the window above the sink.

'No...' Edith whispered.

The third room was the same as the second—and first—except now the dust had turned to a thick, dark blanket and the window that had been boarded was cracked; deep welts in the wood around its frame looked like the narrow pits that nails had been dug into. As if this was the very same window, the boards removed from it. The glass was split; a cool breeze came in and rolled over the tiles. Some were splintered at the edges, she saw, and the table was bruised in the middle by a dark stain. Something had died on it. A trail of ichor oozed over the floor from the table to the corner of the kitchen; something else had dragged the dead thing away.

The door across the room was marked *Food Store*, but the words were old and faded.

'Chaps!' she called, keeping her eyes on the

door. 'There's something weird going on here...'

She moved toward the door. She had walked the entire length of the face, she knew; she *had* to have done. It was impossible. This door must lead outside—and yet—

She lifted the latch and pulled it open. The hinges complained.

The next room was the same. Older, darker, all manner of debris and clumps of filth having streamed in through the open window and littered the place. The tiles on one wall had been ripped away, leaving it wounded and bleeding drywall onto the floor.

Across the room was a door. Above it, a sign that had once read *Food Store*, but now read *oo St e*.

She crossed the room, moving past a table that had started to sag. Opened the pantry door.

The kitchen through this door was a pit of mould and decay; the bones of a deer lay beneath the table. A sheet of what looked like glossy black paper had been attached to the window to cover the hole, but it had torn through; light flared through a peppering of holes and lit the moss and lichen growing on the walls.

Through the next door, she saw death.

The kitchen had been renovated; the tiles were all white, the table replaced by a marble worktop—an island in the middle of the room. It had all been scrubbed, reworked; the cupboards were all locked.

Knives and cleavers hung from the ceiling, all polished and shining. The window was repaired.

It would have gleamed, were it not covered with blood.

It drooled and flowed across every surface, ran down every wall. Slabs of meat were strung up against the far wall; the door marked *Food Store*—now in the red, scrawled handwriting of a madman—was locked too.

There were restraints on the marble surface. Thick, leather bands with buckles. A butcher's apron hung on the wall to her right. Stained with blood.

Edith's eyes widened as she saw the man in the corner of the room.

'Oh, sh—'

And then he was moving towards her, his footsteps heavy; he moved fast, despite his size—Christ, he was *huge*, and was that a *boar's skull* on top of his shoulders?—and she moaned, scrambling behind her for the door—

He swiped at her as she found the handle, and there was a cleaver in his gloved hand, and he was wearing all white and he *stunk* of meat—

The handle twisted as she ducked out of reach—the man wearing the boar's skull and the red apron grunted, thrust the cleaver down, missing her shoulder by inches—

The door opened—

And she fell through, tumbling backwards, twisting her body to slam it closed before the giant could come through after her. Her heart pounded in her throat, her whole body shivering. 'Jesus,' she whispered, 'Jesus, Christ fucking Jesus godfuckingfuckit—'

'Edie?' Abram said behind her.

She whirled around, eyes wide.

Abram and Michael stood at the kitchen table, pinning Charlie to it. Morgan had crossed the room and was poring through one of the cupboards, presumably looking for some kind of medication. Or food. Christ, she'd been hungry before, but now her appetite...

'What's in there?' Abram said, nodding toward the door.

Edith's eyes travelled the room. The kitchen, as it had been when she'd left it the first time. No dust, no deterioration; she'd imagined it all.

Extreme stress, she thought. 'Nothing,' she whispered.

Morgan stood, crossed the room towards her. He was limping, she noticed. 'Let me—'

'Nothing,' she said firmly, gripping the latch. She'd expected to hear thumping, to feel the giant's fists on the wood behind her— but there was no sound.

Morgan looked her in the eyes for a moment, then nodded. 'All right.'

'No, it's not,' Michael grunted, nodding Morgan over to the table. 'Here, hold this bastard's wriggly little legs. I'm having a look.'

'No—' Edith tried, but it was useless.

Michael shoved past her, grabbing the latch and shoving her aside as he swung the door open. 'No, don't—'

'What?' he scowled, snatching the sulphur matches from her. 'It's just a pantry.'

FKKASH

Edith turned, almost sure she could feel the muscles in her neck creaking with the effort. Cautiously, she looked.

The pantry walls were stocked with food. Crooked, wooden shelves lined up with cans and bags of flour. The flickering light illuminated a washing bucket, tools against the far wall; the cupboard was barely six-by-six across, but it seemed to have been filled with every kind of food and utensil imaginable. Meat hung from the ceiling; she shivered.

'And there's what we're looking for,' Michael said, nodding toward the opposite wall. Glass bottles glinted green in the light. 'No bandages, but some of the good stuff ought to help with the pain.' Quickly, he lit another match and made to step forward—

And Edith grabbed him around the waist,

yanked him back. 'Don't!' she yelled.

'What in bloody Christ's name are you—' Michael started, swinging at her.

'Look!' she said, letting go of him. She pointed down.

The floor of the pantry had been carved out, the tiles broken and cracked at the edges of a gaping hole. A deep, black pit that took up most of the entire floor—a single step forward would have sent him tumbling down through the opening.

'Jesus...' Michael whispered.

'What is it?' Abram called from the table.

Edith shook her head. Looked at Michael. He looked back at her. 'It's wrong,' she said. 'This place is all wrong.' Or I'm going mad, she thought.

No, she thought, not if Michael sees it too.

Either we're *all* mad, or there's something about this place that's so far wrong it nearly sent one of us falling right down into Hell.

CHAPTER SIX
MORGAN'S WAY

Young Charlie had finally stopped twitching. His sleep was almost peaceful, his eyelids fluttering only a little as whatever dreams of death and battle plagued him in slightly duller colours than before.

'I have to find a bathroom,' Morgan said after a moment of respite. The others had stepped back from the table; the boy could spend a moment without restraint, it seemed, but still Michael watched him hungrily, as if eager to jump back on the poor kid again.

'Look for bandages while you're out there,' Edith said. 'Laudanum, too, if you find a medicine cabinet.'

'Be careful,' Abram said flatly, but his eyes were pinned to the boy on the table. He wasn't looking at Charlie, Morgan realised, but through him—his mind was elsewhere, miles away. Edith seemed to have noticed too, and she looked warily at him.

'Will do,' Morgan said quietly, and he turned and headed for the kitchen door.

He stepped out into the hallway and closed the door behind him, briefly tipping his head back and letting the dome of his skull rest on the wood. He wasn't desperate for the bathroom; Christ knew he had relieved himself somewhere out there, amid all the smoke and death and blood, though it would be nice to clean himself up and figure out what was wrong with his leg.

No, really, he had just wanted *out*.

He could feel his breath hitching in his throat, his chest tightening. There was a point halfway up his sternum that seemed to project claws into his heart if it begun to pound too fast, too hard, and he focused on that point as though thinking hard enough about it would be enough to stop the bones contracting. His stomach was a knot of nerves and his leg—the good one—was like milk in a ragged cloth sack. His boots were too heavy, he couldn't move, and now he was thinking about his mother and that was the last thing he wanted to do because he should have been thinking about the friends that had died out there, about the young boy on the table who looked familiar—but not enough for him to know the lad's name—or the Nowhere Boys or the house—

How about you just stop thinking altogether? he told himself, and then everything shut down. His bowels trembled and he wanted to cry and he realised he'd been breathing in short, ragged puffs and he could almost *see* her now, that sympathetic droop in her eyes—could she see him? was that why his mother was appearing to him now, because she knew they'd lost and that he was trapped?—and his heart was going a million beats a minute, except a part of him thought it must have stopped completely—

And then his eyes snapped open. He focused on his breathing first. Slow it down, slow it right down—no, now you're going the wrong way, now you're *scared* and that's not going to help—that's it, slow down...

And push it all the way through your body, through your chest, through your belly and into your knees, push...

Push...

And then he saw flashes. A man's head exploded inside his helmet, muck and filth spraying the ground, muck and filth that were as red as rose petals, and the body crumpled. He heard the roar of musket fire and sunk to his knees. Morgan was there again, right there on the battlefield, reaching for his gun but it was gone, scrambling in the dirt for a pike, for a knife, for something—and then his fingers were clasped around something soft and bloody and he realised it was an ear, and he screamed and his breath had sped right up again—

'Stop,' he whispered, closing his eyes again as if that would shut out the visions. '*Stop...*'

Slow. He pushed cautiously at his breathing, trying to loosen the muscles in his legs so that it could pass through them into his feet. Laying a hand on his chest, he splayed out his fingers, trying to stop the clawed centre of his sternum from poking into his heart.

And he counted. One, two, three...

Twelve, thirteen...

A minute. He opened his eyes again, back in the room, almost sweating from exertion, his long, dark hair tugging gently at his scalp. He stood, shaky. His bad leg throbbed.

'You're okay,' he whispered. 'You're all right...'

For the first time since leaving the kitchen, he took in his surroundings. He was back in the entrance hall, and everything was largely the same, except the front door had gone. He crossed the hard, wooden floorboards, heading toward the opposite side of the room, ignoring the tall, dark staircase to his left and the niggling in his brain. There had to be a bathroom through one of these doors, he thought, reaching for the first—

Except the front door had gone.

Morgan froze, turning his head toward the front of the house. His blood ran as cold as ice and he wished for the smoke and blood of outside, for the warmth of a throbbing, twitching body laying across his chest. No, this wasn't right, something was missing, something was *wrong*...

Moving slowly into the middle of the room, Morgan eyed up the space in the wall where the wooden front door had been. He remembered it; the wood had been old and the knots almost marbled into some kind of organic pattern, and there had been a carving in the panels: a hungry mouth, with sharp, pointed teeth, open wide...

And now it was gone.

'Fellas?' he called, keeping his eyes on the wall. The brickwork was old and crumbling—which was odd, since the architecture and materials seemed something that must have been dreamed up centuries from now—and it looked for all the world as though there had never been a door there at all. 'Fellas...'

He turned back to the kitchen door. Maybe he had gone through the wrong exit, maybe he was in another room, maybe he was crazy—

The kitchen door was gone. His heart pounded. Blood throbbed in his ears. He rushed to the wall, confident he was looking at the exact spot where the door had been, confident that he was *standing* where it had been. The room was closing in around him. He was trapped. As good as dead, and god, he wished to be outside. 'Fellas!'

He pounded on the wall where the door had been, first with one fist then with both.

'Open up!' Morgan screamed desperately. 'Open up, for Christ's sake!'

Staggering back, he shook his head. Exhaustion wracked his chest. God, he was going to break down again—shock, he reminded himself, he was in shock—oh, bollocks, what if he died of fright?

Morgan whirled around to face the door he'd been heading toward, the door he'd been sure must lead through to a bathroom.

Gone.

Glancing all around the hallway, he saw that they'd all gone. He remembered three doorways on the kitchen side, and... a couple, at least, on the other. Surely, he told himself, surely I can't have imagined all that.

You're insane, he thought. Remember where you were. Close your eyes. You were in the hallway, heading for a door. You thought there might be a room through there.

That doesn't seem an unreasonable assumption.

And you were thinking about how the Nowhere Boys scare you, in a weird kind of way that you can't quite place—like they shouldn't *be*, like they're not right—and about how the house, this house, scares you even more, and... why? Just a feeling, an impulse? Or an instinct?

And now, when you open your eyes, all the doors will be...

Gone. He looked. The walls were plain.

And closer.

'What...'

He backed up. Bumped the wall behind him. With a start, he turned toward the staircase. It loomed, a spiralling passageway into unknown, clouded depths of inky black above. It hadn't changed at all. But everything else...

He crossed the room to where the front door had been. Some cruel trick, he thought. Someone else was here, someone who'd papered over it while they'd fussed over Charlie. Some malicious bastard who—

There was a shuddering *creak* and the front wall rumbled as it started gliding towards him.

'What the Cavalier-fucking *shit*...'

His head spun. The back wall beckoned darkly. The stairs...

The floor shook. He nearly toppled over, glanced to his right—the second wall was coming in, sliding forward as though on runners. The hallway was tightening.

'No!' he yelled, turning toward the kitchen—

The wall smacked him in the face. The hallway was a narrow corridor, trembling and shaking and batting him left and right, and now the front wall was closer, grinding across the floorboards, closer, closer...

'Shit,' he said, stumbling toward the stairs.

CHAPTER SEVEN
THE GENERAL

Oliver Abram was miles away. He was in a room with the man himself. Their hero, their leader, a man only few had been privileged enough to meet. Cromwell was shorter than he'd expected. And he was giving orders. Complicated ones—they made sense, sure, but was this the right thing to do?—and Abram simply nodded. He was a soldier, not a thinker. What was right didn't matter anymore. Nothing really did.

There came a muffled yell from outside the kitchen and he jolted out of the hazy half-memory. The lights dimmed. Flickered. The boy on the table was still. 'What was that?' he murmured.

From across the table, Michael Caldwell glared at him. 'What?'

'Someone out in the hall,' Abram said. 'How long's that Morgan chap been gone?'

'A few minutes,' Edith frowned. 'But... I don't hear anything.'

'Keep an eye on him,' Abram said, nodding toward the young man on the table. 'If he stirs, call for me.'

'Boss,' Michael grunted.

Abram looked at him, hard. 'Something you want to say, Shuck?'

Michael was silent, but his eyes said enough. His face was spotted with soot and pale with malnourishment; his pupils burned as brightly as they ever had.

'Thought as much,' Abram said quietly, and he turned to leave the room. 'Look after the boy.'

He stepped out into the hall, leaving the door open.

'We need to talk about the boss,' Michael said quietly.

Edith glanced toward the open door. confident that Abram had not heard, she nodded. 'We do,' she whispered.

The hallway was a swamp of thin, grey mist. For a moment Abram thought that the fog and smoke from outside must have broken in through cracks in the wall, that the outside was coming in, but no: as he stood there, up to his waist in slowly blossoming clouds of grey, he realised that it was dust. That it had been disturbed—perhaps by their entry into the house, perhaps by something else—and that now the light coming in through the tall, wide windows either side of the front door was illuminating it, throwing shafts of grey and white onto each speck so that plumes of "mist" formed and rolled across the floor.

'Morgan?' he called softly, glancing across the hall. Everything was as he remembered; doors on each side of the hall, all closed. The front door, a marvel made of the kind of rich, dark wood he'd only seen used for ships' hulls. 'Morgan, boy, are you out here?'

He saw a light on in another room, bleeding around the edges of the door in thin, spindly beams. The same kind of unnatural light that he'd seen in every room in this house, flickering not in the manner of a candle or a matchlight but in an almost artificial, juddering way. Morgan must have been in there, he thought, though he couldn't hear anything from beyond the door. Still, there was no sign of him out here; whatever thumping sound he'd heard had been in his imagination. Perhaps he was, as Michael Caldwell suspected, going mad; oh, he was not so naïve as to be oblivious to the younger man's suspicions, not so dumb as to not notice the wary looks or the sideways glares.

Abram turned to step back into the kitchen, but stopped. Something on the floor, just by the foot of the stairs.

If he'd have looked up, he'd have seen a dark shape slip into the shadows at the top of the stairs; but he did not look up, and he did not see Morgan, and instead bent down to pick up the ragged slip of parchment from the floor. A note.

Try the library, it read, in a clipped, incursive kind of handwriting that seemed so very out of place, even in this house that was entirely so.

'The library,' he murmured, stuffing the note into his uniform. Brushing himself down, he realised that the dust swirling around him had begun to clump and gather on the material; or was it just caked filth from outside? Christ, that all seemed so long ago now, as if they'd been in here for years—it couldn't have been more than an hour, but already time seemed to have moved on and left them behind.

He heard Michael and Edith whispering and looked up toward the open kitchen door. 'Is that boy all right in there?' he called. Shadows twisted and writhed in the gap between door and frame. Neither of them answered, and he stepped forward. 'I say, is that boy—'

The door slammed shut, disturbing a cloud of sooty dust that billowed around him, almost forcefully enough to shove him back.

Anger flared and pulsed like thunder at the back of his skull. 'I say,' he called again, storming toward the door. He hammered on the wood, twisted at the knob. 'Michael, you bastard—'

Distraction. Movement. Off to his left. He looked—

The window. Something had flitted past it.

Cautiously, the slamming door forgotten, Abram moved toward the tall window and stood in the grey, shifting glare of the light beyond the glass. Looking out across the field, he saw a ribbon of dark trees spreading across the horizon; a mile and a half away, at best, and yet it seemed so far from them.

Sighing, Abram leant on the sill and watched the world moving outside. Tall, unkempt knots of grass twitched and swayed gently in the breeze. The smoke from the battlefield on the hill had begun to drift down and now it slipped through the blades of grass like an invading force, rolling gently between clumps of earth, disturbing the ground, almost dripping with blood.

He wondered, briefly, if he could remember this window being here before. But his memory was not what it had been, and so he supposed it didn't matter particularly either way.

Something moved at the tree-line.

'You *bastards*,' he muttered, squinting into the dark. He saw shadows slipping between the trees, like the smoke through the grass. He saw the orange sparks of a fire, and his eyes moved up, up, to the canopy of the forest. A thick plume of rigid, white smoke slipped into the clouds like the breath of some dying beast on its back. He heard them too, laughing and plotting, their voices carrying on the wind.

They were out there. Fucking Royalists. He wondered if they could see him, too, looking out at them through the glass. He ducked back, pressed himself against the wall. It didn't matter, he thought. whether they could see him or not, they were coming for the house. There was nothing else out here; it made *sense* to attack the unnatural, gothic building that had appeared out of nowhere. It made sense for them to come here.

Abram and his men were running out of time.

'Chaps,' he said, moving to the kitchen door again, 'we need to—'

He frowned. Another note was pinned to the wood. It hadn't been there a moment ago, he was certain of it.

There was someone else in here with them. Someone was playing games with them. He thought of calling out, of yelling for this strange, silent figure to show themselves, but already he was reading the note:

Nowhere else is safe.

The same scrawled handwriting, only this time the ink was red. The note smelled of pennies. His brow wrinkled. 'Nowhere *else* is safe?'

He shook his head, plucking the note from the door and stuffing it into his shirt. His fingers brushed the first scrap of paper, and he remembered.

Try the library.

They weren't two separate notes, he realised, but two parts of the same written warning:

Try the library. Nowhere else is safe.

'Chaps,' he said, a little louder, going for the doorknob. He turned it. Locked. 'Michael—Edith—if you two are playing silly buggers, you can just—'

Something behind him. Coughing. He turned.

Across the hall, the beads of light around the edge of the closed door had turned red. They flickered still, in that same unnatural manner, but now the candleflame—or whatever it was—was a deep, bloody shade. Shadows moved in the narrow crack between door and frame. The light pulsed and bent. A harrowing, dry coughing was coming from behind the door.

'Morgan?' Abram said, moving slowly for the door. 'Are you all right in there, son?'

Nowhere else is safe.

Nowhere but the library. But how would they know which door belonged to the library? He remembered the sign above the pantry in the kitchen, the sign that read *Food Store.* His eyes flitted up, to the space above the door in front of him.

A thin, scratchy Catholic cross had been carved into the wall. The crossbeam was too low down; it looked like the crucifix had been flipped upside-down.

He stood by the door and listened. The coughing had faded. Now, whoever was in there was moaning.

The red light flashed, once, and then he heard glass shatter. The light disappeared, fizzling out, fading to orange and then vanishing and leaving the crack between door and frame threaded through with blackness. A thick, seeping cold crept out through the wood and chilled him. When he exhaled, his breath came out in a thin white plume.

'Morgan?'

Silence. Darkness.

Abram reached out gingerly and laid his hand on the octagonal knob of the door. The iron was cold, cold enough that he recoiled.

Grasping it firmly, he twisted. A soft *click*. The door was locked. He twisted the other way. *Click*. 'Morgan?'

He stepped back, glanced toward the kitchen door. Still closed.

Cree—eeek...

Abram swallowed, turned back to the locked door. It stood open, beckoning. He saw nothing through the doorway, nothing but shadows. And a faint, red pinprick of light, in the distance—too distant to be inside the room, but perhaps there was a window...

'Morgan?' he whispered, and he stepped through the door and into the dark.

CHAPTER EIGHT
THE BUTCHER'S TABLE (II)

Ghoulish red light streamed in through the windows. He was in a church of blood, the glass stained with it, slops of meat dripping across the panes, greasy pink smears of entrails painted across each panel by thick-fingered hands. Charlie groaned as he tried to roll over. the bonds digging into his wrists strained. Leather. Buckles. His eyes snapped wide open.

'Where...' he tried, but the stench of liver and lungs filled his throat and he coughed, wet chunks shooting out of his mouth. Was that his own blood, or—

A shiver of pain coursed through his body and he convulsed. Yeah. It was his own blood.

'*Where...*'

A shadow moved in the corner of the room.

Charlie's head snapped up as he tried to sit upright, tried to look toward the shape, but he couldn't twist himself enough to see. His stomach bled wetly into his hands. The bonds were more like straps, he found; he had a certain radius of movement, but he couldn't reach the left buckle with his right hand, or vice versa. That would be too easy. Each one was just out of reach, just by half an inch...

'Huhh huhh huhh,' something grunted. It wasn't laughter, no, it was something sick and sad. But there was a cruelty in those odd, beastly moans, one that Charlie recognised. One he'd seen on the battlefield; whatever was in this room with him, it was going to *enjoy* this...

'Help me,' Charlie said, letting his head fall back onto the table. 'Please... I'll tell you everything. I'll tell you what they're planning...'

The shadow moved over him. Charlie looked up and saw that it really *was* a shadow; he heard clomping, leaden footsteps and deduced, from those and the shuddering movements of the shade on the ceiling, that the beast was moving toward him but that its shadow extended long before it; it was tall, unnaturally so, too tall to be human...

He craned his neck, strained his eyes to one side. He saw the approaching figure and his heart thumped the top of his throat. 'No, listen to me,' he begged, tugging with both fists as pain surged through his stomach and a jet of blood arced out of him. 'Please...'

The butcher came close. Flies buzzed around the giant's masked face. He wore a long, striped apron—blue and white, vertical, although it was hard to tell with all the flecks of wet black and the deep, brown stains—and a canvas shirt and trousers that had once been white but were now a deep, pooled red. He was a good seven feet tall—taller, maybe—and his shoulders were as wide as the table Charlie was strapped too was long. He was colossal, a monolithic structure of blood and blades. His sleeves were rolled up and his arms were thick as pillars. In his left, he clutched the handle of a sharp, glinting cleaver.

He wore a pig's skull over his face. Bigger than any pig Charles Buxton had ever seen;

this man's face was hidden behind the dead, hollow eye sockets of a wild boar. A hog of monstrous proportions.

'No,' Charlie said. 'No...'

He struggled. Looking straight down his own body, he could just see his musket at the very end of the table—it had been laid between his legs, out of reach, to taunt him—and another pair of thick, leather braces around his ankles. Charlie pulled and yanked at the bands, kicking and thrashing, each movement squeezing more blood from the hole in his abdomen, and he heard that sound again:

'*Huhhh huhhh huhhhhh...*'

The stink of meat was unbearable, the buzzing of flies like the roaring of cannon fire in every direction. There were hundreds of them, a Biblical swarm, and now he saw there were wet piles of meat in the corners and at the edges of the room, thick slabs laid over twitching coils of pink rope.

The butcher stood over him, brandishing the cleaver. He tipped the blade slowly back and forth and Charlie watched, frozen in place, as the bloody light dripped across the silver edges in beautiful, shimmering pools. Being in this room was like being underwater. Everything was muffled and muted, separated from normality by the surface far above—but that surface was red and screaming.

No. The screaming was coming from him.

Charlie kicked out suddenly, catching the barrel of the musket and sending the gun skittering into his other leg. He tried to coil his foot around, to curl his toes around the stock, but in his manic thrashing he knocked the musket off the table. It clattered, bounced, skidded through something soft.

'No!' Charlie yelled as the butcher raised his weapon, the boar's skull grinning hideously on his shoulders with chipped, broken teeth. Charlie yanked with his left hand, pulling, swinging, fighting the leather—

Something snapped. His shoulder popped loudly as his arm came free and he screamed, but there was no time to register the pain or the fact he might have broken something, and already he was scrambling for the second buckle, wailing like a child as the butcher raised the cleaver—

'Fuck!' Charlie yelled, his fingers wet with sweat and blood, digging madly for the buckle. 'Fuck, come on!'

The cleaver came down.

But that was after.

CHAPTER NINE
A GOOD YEAR

On the clean kitchen table, the half-dead kid twitched. Michael Caldwell cocked an eyebrow, watching for more movement; Charlie was still again.

'Think he's okay, Shuck?' Edith said. She had found a crooked wooden stool at the edge of the room and was sitting beside the table, one hand on his shoulder to keep him pinned down.

'Dreaming,' Michael shrugged, turning his eyes toward the pantry door. 'He'll be fine. Wherever he is in his head, I'm sure it's better than this shithole.'

Edith paused. 'First time you've ever let me call you that without biting my head off,' she said carefully. 'How are *you* doing, Caldwell?'

He didn't answer. She followed his gaze,

looked into the dark storage cupboard. 'You want to go down there, don't you?'

Michael looked back at her. His face had softened, anger replaced by a bristling, electric curiosity. Not softened, she supposed, but shifted. There was a sort of kindness there, but it was just as hard as his fury.

The kitchen door slammed shut. Edith bolted around, staring at it. 'What was—'

Michael shook his head. 'Wind,' he said. They listened for a moment. No wind, and they'd closed the front door when they came in. But neither of them wanted to argue logic. 'Think the general's all right out there?'

Edith hesitated again. 'I don't know if he's all right at all,' she said. 'This mission... it's all wrong, Shuck. I don't know if he can do it.'

'Lucky he's got us at his back, then,' Michael said. 'Because I'll fucking do it.'

Edith looked at him. 'You would?'

He smiled thinly. 'You wouldn't?'

Beneath them, something tinkled. The sound of glass on glass, a toast. Edith swallowed.

'You stay with the boy,' Michael said,

moving to the open pantry door. He stood in the frame for a moment, surveying the cupboard. 'Listen out for Abram. I'm going down there.'

'No, you're not,' Edith said, standing to join him. She laid a hand on his arm, and he didn't shrug it away. Her eyes fell onto the hole in the floor. 'What kind of fool would go down there? Besides, we should stick together.'

Michael grinned. 'We should?'

'Don't be a pillock. For the kid, I mean. You think I'm going to be able to hold him down if he starts moving again?'

'You're stronger than most of the chaps I know,' Michael reasoned.

'You're more of a bastard than everyone I know put together,' Edith said. 'Doesn't mean I wouldn't trust you with my life.'

His smile changed. It was real, now. Rare and unusual, and real. 'Really?'

'Wouldn't you trust me with yours?'

He looked at her. It might have been just for a second, but it felt like much longer. 'Yes,' he said eventually.

'Then trust me now,' she said, squeezing

his arm. 'Don't go down there.'

Michael's eyes returned to the opposite wall. He nodded at something hanging among the shelves. 'Quick trip,' he said. 'Just a minute. Just to see.'

Edith looked. Hanging on the pantry wall was a long coil of rope, the threads fused together with tar. One end was frayed, the other tied into a hangman's knot. Must have been eighteen or twenty yards long.

'No,' she said. 'Stay with me. With the kid.'

Michael ignored her, leaning forward to grab the rope.

'Careful, idiot, you'll—'

Michael slipped, nearly wheeling forward and right into the ragged hole in the floor. Edith's grip on his arm tightened and she yanked back sharply, dragging him back into the kitchen.

'Jesus, Caldwell, are you trying to fucking fall down there?'

He grunted. 'Hold on,' he said stubbornly, tensing his arm in her grip. With the fingers of one hand curled tightly around the doorframe, he stepped forward, right to the edge of the hole, and leaned as far into the pantry as possible, stretching his arm to the wall—

'Got it,' he said, snagging the rope and falling back, pulling it off the wall.

Edith nodded. 'Great,' she said, staring down into the hole in the floor. 'Now what, dog-brain? What are you going to do, drop down there and...'

He raised an eyebrow. 'And?'

Edith's eyes were locked on the shadows beneath the deep well in the ground. Something had moved down there. Something big.

She looked up at him.

'Don't go down there,' she said. 'Please.'

'I'm going down there.'

'You're not,' Edith said. 'You're not going to go down there and leave me up here and make sure we both definitely die—'

'Oh, I'm absolutely going to go down there,' Michael said, pointing at the hole.

'You're not!'

'I really think I'm going down there.'

'You're—Christ, you're frustrating—fine!'

Edith seethed. 'Fine. But if you're going to be a silly bollocks, you can go down yourself.'

'Will you at least help me down?' Michael said.

'No.'

'Not even a little bit?'

'Not even a—what are you, Shuck, a fucking child?—you want to go down into the death hole, you go by yourself.'

'Death hole?'

'Death hole. Go on then, idiot.'

Michael looked up. His eyes passed between three thick, clawed hooks embedded in the ceiling. Meathooks, he supposed. 'Easy as pie,' he said.

'Well, let's hope whatever's down there doesn't turn you into one,' Edith scowled, returning to the table.

The cellar was a cavern hewn roughly from the foundations, the walls brown rock and clay that looked as though they might come crumbling down, if not for the wooden struts and supports crisscrossing them. As Michael lowered himself in through the hole in the basement's ceiling, he saw that the whole place was lit: a soft, pulsing amber light guided him down to the floor.

His feet touched the ground and he shifted his weight warily, letting go of the rope and letting it dangle beside him. The floor beneath him was not concrete or wood, or even the strange tiles of the kitchen; it was just earth, tightly packed, coated in dust. Solid enough, if a little spongy. This was the first familiar thing he'd found in this damn house.

'Edie?' he called up, looking up into the food store. The jagged edges of the hole bled with the light of a candle he'd lit above; orange pooled through and stroked the highest threads of the rope that he'd strung up through the meathooks. He gave the rope a quick tug, jerking it down roughly. Nothing. Solid.

'You good down there, shithead?' Edith called.

'Why, missing me already?' he called back.

Edith's shadow disappeared from the edge of the hole. Michael grinned to himself and pulled on the rope again, just to make sure. Above him, one of the meathooks jangled; the rope remained.

Satisfied, he moved forward into the cellar.

Lanterns hung from the walls, illuminating the earthen face of each with a soft throb of yellow at regular intervals. Patches of light seeped over the floor, but long shadows still drew in from each corner and from the rough edges of the room. It was large; even the lit portion was three or four times the size of the kitchen, and Michael could tell that there was more he couldn't see. The walls didn't just disappear in the darkness, but faded into it, pitch-black areas spreading far beyond his comprehension.

'What have you got for me?' he whispered, walking slowly through the dust. Thick, rectangular beams supported the high ceiling, spaced out in some labyrinthine pattern so that he had to duck around one to see past another. Along the nearest wall, huge, oaken barrels were stacked atop one another. Each one must have contained eight or nine gallons, and there were dozens. All plugged with wide, rubber stoppers and sealed. There were markings on each barrel, some of which made no sense.

Honey & Orange. 1862

For John. 1494

Raspberry Blend. 2012

On one, the words "Dublin, 57%. 1913" had been scratched out with a thick, dripping red line. In their place, someone had written in the same weeping red legend:

Library. Only chance.

'Whiskey,' Michael grinned, moving toward the barrels.

Something skittered behind him.

Michael whirled around, his blood running cold and freezing him in place. He peered into the dark of the cellar, ears almost twitching as he listened for that quiet scuttling again. He nearly called out, but there was nothing there. He'd imagined it.

Just as he was about to turn back to the whiskey barrels, he saw a glint in the farthest corner of the cellar. Flaring beads of light rippling off a curved glass surface. Beside it, another; they looked like the flashing eyes of a deer in the dark.

'Hello...' Michael whispered. Turning, he moved to the wall and wrestled with the bracket holding a lit lantern in place. The flame inside the greasy glass cage fluttered as he ripped it down and turned again.

When he looked into the dark, the glint had gone. 'No,' he said quietly, pressing forward a little. 'Where are—ah, there you are.'

He moved between two pillars, squinting into the shadows. The glinting thing seemed further from him than before, but that could only mean there were more of them. That was *good*.

The light spread before him in pulsing circles, and as the glow from the lights behind him faded back and he stepped into the dark, the soft throb of the lamp in his hand became his only source. He looked back over his shoulder: the rope was still hanging there. Everything was fine.

When he turned back, the glinting object had disappeared again. He looked left and right, swinging the lantern in a wide, slow arc. There, off to his right. Three or four of them, shining like glass. They had been directly in front of him before; had he disoriented himself that badly?

'Here we go,' he whispered, keeping his eyes on the flaring patches of light as he pressed into the dark. The lantern flickered. 'Oh, *look* at you...'

The wine rack stretched across an entire wall and seemed to curl around a far corner, too; there must have been hundreds of bottles here, if not thousands. Setting the lantern on the dusty ground, Michael stepped up to the nearest rack and reached up. The bottles were all laid on their sides, corked throats poking out from a crisscrossed wire shelving unit. Green glass and white, and the smell...

He pulled a bottle, dislodging a plume of dust. Coughing, he read, *Tula, 1883*. Eager, careless hands wrestled with the cork and sent it flying with a *pop!*. Raising the bottle to his nose, he took in a long whiff and his brain warmed instantly. The room seemed to soften. Oh, this was good wine.

He read the label more closely. Thirteen per cent alcohol by volume; "good for dinner parties". He drank.

Warm, sweet wine slid down his throat and his chest opened up to accommodate. The smell was fruity and obnoxious; he took a deep gulp and shoved the soggy, crumbled cork back into the neck, sliding the bottle into the rack.

Knok knok knok

Michael spun round, looking back toward the barrels. A scrawny shape slithered away from them and into the dark.

A rat, he supposed.

Rats don't knock, a small part of his brain warned him, but the rest was fuzzy and enamoured and he returned to the wine rack unconcerned about whatever might be down here in the dark. What was it Edith had said, as he was lowering himself down the rope? Something about seeing a shape moving down here? It didn't matter. There was *wine*.

Still, as he reached for another bottle with one hand, he patted the thigh of his uniform, making sure his knife was still tucked into his belt.

The next was a white, and a good one. He

drank a little and spat the rest. Tasting etiquette.

Something chirruped in the dark. Freezing with a bottle of Spanish red pressed to his mouth, Michael listened. A bird? Perhaps one had gotten into the house through the chimney, fallen into the cellar through the hole in the pantry floor...

Claws scraped over the soft earth behind him and he swallowed, lowering the bottle.

'Hello?' he said softly, turning his head to scour the patchy dark of the cellar.

Nothing.

He shrugged, raising the bottle again.

He didn't hear the scratch of claws on grass or the *tink* of something crawling across the top of the wine rack. All he heard was the shuddering *glub-glub-glub* of the bottle as it poured sweet, dark honey into his throat.

Something smashed.

Michael spun around, dropping the bottle. The shatter of glass echoed around him as a plume of dust exploded at his ankles and red mist splashed his legs. Tiny shards of green glass showered the floor.

And he saw it.

Perched on top of the wine rack, a creature the size of a badger glared at him with sunken yellow eyes. Its figure was largely in shadow but Michael saw spindly, bony arms and legs, and a ribbon of pulsing tumours spreading across its throat and shoulder.

'Oh, shit,' he said, backing away.

Knok knok knok

He looked across at the barrels and saw two more of the creatures, climbing up the stacks to the top where they crawled over each other, knuckles rapping the wood. Both heads turned toward him at once.

Another bottle smashed as the creature behind him leapt at his back. Michael cried out as claws raked his shoulder and turned around, staggering backward, his movements swaying and bending as if he'd just stepped off a boat. He felt he was going to vomit; he glanced toward the rope, fumbling for his knife, suddenly on his knees and crawling—

'No!' he yelled as the creature swiped at his leg, launching a fist down toward its head. It screeched and dipped aside and his knuckles ploughed into the earthy floor. 'You little shit!'

Stumbling to his feet, he wheeled towards the rope, batting away another of the creatures as it lunged for him from the shadows. Its flank was covered in boils, in the same wet, raw blisters that decorated the first. Ragged clumps of fur matted its brown, leathery skin. As he elbowed it in the throat and sent it sprawling, another came at his ankle, clawed at his flesh through the material of his uniform.

'Edith!' he yelled, slipping between two pillars—were they closer together now?—to get to the dangling rope. 'Edith, help me up!'

He saw more of them now, crawling over the barrels at the far end of the room. Half a dozen at least, perching on kegs and watching him, clawing at the wood in excitement. One was missing an eye and the socket was wet with jelly and pus. One's jaw had snapped and hung loose from a slavering, grey tongue.

One leapt for him—he felt a movement in the air and ducked—and it soared over his head and smacked a pillar. Instantly it dug its claws in and coiled around the wooden beam, coming for him again; this time it landed on Michael's chest, knocking him back. He yelled, tipping his head back as it came at his throat with tiny, pointed teeth snapping in its little maw. With both fists he smashed the thing's round, chittering skull. A wet *crunch* echoed as he reached the rope, grabbed it with both hands, started to climb—

He was almost halfway up when claws grabbed his ankle and started to pull.

CHAPTER TEN
THE FAMILY

Edith never heard the screaming. She should have; she was well within range of the hole, and the acoustics in the cellar were enough to carry Michael's voice up to her. But the very moment he begun to venture away from the rope and into the shadows, something happened to the hole in the floor.

If she'd tried to follow him down, she'd have found that the hole had closed itself off. It still *looked* like it was there—the ragged edges had not fused together or spread into the centre—but if she'd have tried to push even her foot in through the opening, she'd have found a solid floor beneath it. If she'd tried to pull the rope, she'd have found it anchored, as though whatever invisible surface had closed over the hole had trapped it there too. The hole was no more than an illusion, a painting on the floor through which there was no passage.

But Edith did not discover any of this—not that the hole had been filled in with some unseeable material, nor that the rope had been practically severed—because she never heard the screaming.

Edith watched the boy for a while and, satisfied that his pain was at least giving him some respite in whatever deep sleep he'd been granted—for now, at least—begun to explore the kitchen. First grabbing her pike from where she'd left it on the counter, she looked again through all the cupboards. There was no denying that the house was abandoned; if the dust covering every surface wasn't enough to give that away, the fact that there was no food or drink in here should have been. Still, she couldn't shake the feeling that she was being watched. Not necessarily by something in the house, but—somehow— by the house itself, as though the walls had eyes and the windows were not clear panes of glass but mirrors reflecting a false world, and behind them something was gazing in at her.

Turning, she looked across the floor, frowning thoughtfully at the pink-and-blue tiles. There was no apparent pattern or conscious decision behind their placement; they were random, like panels in a dull and simplistic stained-glass window or a huge mosaic of which she could only view a tiny part. Was the blue the tiled iris of an enormous, watchful eye, and the scattered pink some kind of sickness?

From here, though, there seemed to be... something. As though their placement was not as random as it had seemed from the other side of the room. Cocking her head to one side, she noted that the pink tiles seemed to bloom in a particular direction, and that the more she leaned, the thicker the line they formed. A straight line, pointing away from her...

She took another step, closing one eye. If she bent down a little, the line straightened further still, and now she saw that the clusters of pink tiles in the corner of the room had formed an arrowhead, come together in triangular formation to point to... the wall.

She frowned, walking along the length of the arrow. As she moved, the shape disappeared; just by moving a couple of feet, she found that the arrow had become distorted and spread wide. A couple more, and it had vanished altogether.

She glanced back in Charlie's direction, watching him carefully for a moment. The boy was fine. Wasn't going anywhere. Wasn't her problem.

She turned back to the wall, certain that this was the portion the arrow had been pointing toward. But there was nothing here. Gingerly, she brushed the wall with her fingers—and the pad of her index brushed over a gentle crease. She paused, turned back her hand to find it again. There. A seam, hair-width and invisible.

She traced the outline of a door—up, right, down—and stepped back. There was no discoloration across the wall, nothing to give it away; yet, there it was.

Gently, she pushed.

Click.

The world behind her exploded.

Edith's ears rang as she whirled around, stumbling back until she hit the wall, her eyes already big and wide and terrified. The sound was incredible. She made to say something as she saw Charlie's eyes snap open, but there was no time. The next few seconds played out as though they'd be the last she'd experience; as though whatever cruel god had smacked this malicious shell of a house into the ground—right here, right now—had decided to grant her some relief in her last moments by stretching them out across eternities.

Or perhaps it was taunting her, giving her the opportunity to reach out, to change things in those unbelievably long seconds, and yet fusing her legs to the floor with molten iron.

Either way, she thought she was pretty much fucked when the wall exploded before her.

The pantry door had slammed shut with a crash so loud she was amazed the old wood—

for it *was* old, even though it seemed to have been crafted with tools far more advanced than any she'd encountered—hadn't splintered. And now it swung open again, and her gaze shifted to the space beyond the door, and she saw that it was black. The food store was gone, and the swirling, writhing shadows in its place were thick and choked with a dripping, glistening inky darkness.

And then the door blew off its hinges and the wall erupted in a volcanic scream of white-pink dust and rubble. Edith's hands were raised in front of her face before she'd even thought to duck, but still she heard the boy on the table cry out in fear as brick and stone shattered into the room. Edith blinked, looked in the direction of the explosion, and through the ragged, wasted hole that had been a tiled wall she saw the *other* kitchen.

The old kitchen, the one she'd walked through before, filled with dust and shadows.

'What...'

And then there was a horrific shriek of wood on ceramic, of fingernails on a rough stone surface, of grating church doors on an unholy night, and the kitchen table—Charlie still on it—was shunted towards the rupture.

'No!' Edith screamed, lurching forward to grab the table leg. Her fingers brushed wood and she slipped, knocking her knees on the tiled floor. Charlie's face was white as he turned to look at her, to scramble off the table as it flew across the room, shoved by some immense, invisible hand. His eyes betrayed the most fiercely intense fear she'd ever seen, and then he was gone. The table shot into the old kitchen, and even as the rubble and debris started flying back after him, fusing and knitting back together to reform and reshape the wall they'd burst from, she heard the explosion of the next wall, the grinding of table legs on tiles; Charlie shot through the old kitchen into the next one she'd seen, and then something else exploded and his screams were quieter, farther away...

And she remembered the last kitchen she'd seen through there, the farthest version of this awful room; the butcher's kitchen, the room covered in blood and occupied by the madman with the cleaver—

The wall sealed up, and Edith was alone.

For a moment she tried to catch her breath, holding her chest with one hand to try and compress it, to slow her beating heart. 'Where...' she whispered, and then she lost her voice. The wall was as it had been, as if it had never erupted, as if the pieces hadn't been scattered across the floor just moments ago. The only sign that anything had happened at all was a pair of straight, black smears across the tiles, where the table had shot across them so far that it had burned through the ceramic. She wondered if the legs were on fire, wherever he was now.

She knew where he was now, and her heart almost stopped at the thought. He was in that room, that smeared-red room, with *him*...

And Edith was alone.

She tried the door into the main hallway, calling for Morgan and Abram, but neither of them answered. Perhaps the demon in possession of this house—for that was what she was certain it must be, some wooden-legged demon, or some witch—had shunted them away too, exploding walls and reforming them after, trapping everyone in separate bloody corners of the manor, splitting them up, isolating them. Preparing them. For... what?

She tried the pantry door. No luck there, either, and nothing from Michael when she called for him.

For a while she sat huddled on the floor beside the pantry, sobbing tearlessly. Her throat was raw but she moaned as her chest heaved, her entire body shaking. She had never been afraid before, not like this.

And there was no way out. She had tried hammering on the windowpanes, but the glass was thicker than any she'd ever seen, *inches* thick. The house had her trapped, too.

Unless...

She remembered, suddenly, the hidden door she'd found. Looking up, she saw it across the room, only slightly ajar. She'd have to bend her body almost in half to fit through it, but it was surely possible.

No, she thought. That was where the house

wanted her to go. The only option it had given her. But... what else could she do? Sit here and weep like an infant until it found some other way to kill her? That was what it wanted to do, she knew so much now. It wanted them all dead.

She had no choice.

Slowly she rose to her feet, breathing steadily through her nose, her teeth gritted. Her bones felt weak and fluid, her limbs hanging off her joints like dead weights. She had dropped her pike. She bent to grab it, and glimpsed firelight through the tiny secret door. The flickering amber of a hearth. And she realised she *was* cold, she was damn near frozen, like the winter all the thatch of her parents' roof had burned through and she'd spent months shivering at night. And it wasn't just *as* cold now, it was *that* cold, as though the house could see into her mind, as though it was playing with her memories.

As she crawled closer to the door, she heard the *pop!* of a burning log. The fire was crackling, and she'd never wanted to be warm more than she did now. Well, perhaps once...

'No,' she whispered, freezing in place.

But there was nowhere else to go.

'Fuck,' she murmured, and she crawled to the door and reached out to push it all the way open.

Squeezing through the door meant pulling in her shoulders, gripping her pike close to her waist and drawing in all the breath she could, and by the time she'd dragged her ankles through the little opening and lurched up onto her feet she was spent. It swung shut behind her with a *click*.

No going back.

Edith swallowed fearfully as the room swam into view in shades of red and gold, hazy as if pieced together from the shards of three or four different dreams. She hoped the floor would open up and she'd plummet through it suddenly; she'd kick herself awake, then, and this would all be over.

But the hardwood beneath her was solid, and the nightmare was far from finished with her.

The living room was decorated with candelabras and elaborate gold frames, thick and gilded with roses; the pictures within them were painted in shades of grey, and looked almost real, like the artist had captured every single grain of detail somehow. They didn't look painted at all, but... taken straight from life itself, moments frozen in time. She saw images across the room of a house like this one, but in one of the paintings it was stood in the middle of some dense, futuristic metropolis; in another, it loomed over the smouldering planes of a desolated wasteland. The same house, but in vastly different settings. Perhaps, even, at different points in time.

In the middle of the room, two red-cushioned armchairs and a chaise lounge, all moulded with the same rose-petal design. The velvet material of the cushions was tattered and dusty. A broken chess set lay on a small, wooden table between all the chairs, abandoned as though the game in progress had been left to be continued later. A roaring fire cracked and sizzled in the heart, thick, knotted logs bubbling and foaming as the sap boiled out of them. To her right—in the wall that *should* have separated this room from the main hall—was a tall, wide window that looked out onto the field outside. She saw the tree-line in the distance, a band of green and black that rippled in the wind.

'Daddy,' said a small voice, 'she's here.'

Edith whipped her head around and her heart skipped a few thousand beats.

The chairs were occupied. A young girl lay on her front on the chaise lounge, her hair ratty and knotted as though she'd just crawled through a filthy tunnel. Her face was greasy and she grinned across the room at Edith, a glass chess piece in her hand. She squeezed, and something cracked loudly. Blood beaded between her fingers and dripped in thick strings onto the carpet.

There was a man in the armchair with its back to Edith; she could see the balding crown of his head. And in the other, her head tipped back, mouth open in a silent scream, was Mother. Her hair, too, was a mess, but it was all sticking up and jutting in every direction like a bird's nest struck by lightning. Her scalp was visible and covered in blisters. Her eyes were wide and unseeing.

The chess board, Edith saw, was covered in a random scattering of pieces; too many to be just the one set. Indeed, she saw some were a polished black, some bone-white, some glass—cracked and bloody, as though the girl had already been through them all and squeezed the life out of them—and some a gritty, scorched stone.

'Can we play with her, Daddy?' said the girl. Her mouth didn't move. Edith squinted. It was stitched up. She was smiling, grinning hungrily, but her lips were sealed. Her eyelids were puckered with black welts; they had been stitched up too, but the twine had been ripped from them. She wore all black.

'I...' Edith said, backing away. She hit the wall and her stomach tipped forward. 'I don't...'

'Daddy, she's afraid,' the girl giggled, her lips twitching with each word. 'Look at her! Look at the whore, Daddy! Look at the whore with her pointy stick!'

Edith's grip tightened on the shaft of the pike.

'Daddy...'

This voice didn't belong to the girl. Edith's eyes shifted toward the hearth and she saw a shadow, half-hidden behind the feet of the father's armchair. An animal shape, fitting and convulsing in the flickering light of the flames. A dog?

'*Hungry...*'

'Daddy, can we?' said the girl.

'*Hungry!*' slobbered the animal hiding at his feet. '*Daddy!*'

'Daddy, *can* we?'

The father raised a slow, bony hand. Three fingers raised, the fourth curled down into a claw. 'Shhh...' he whispered. 'Darling'—there was a loud *click-click-click* as his neck twisted to one side, like the creaking of a tall tree in a gale—'shall we let the children have her?'

Edith opened her mouth.

The mother said nothing. There was a hole in her chest, Edith saw, and an iron poker jammed into it. Sooty handprints—the handprints of a child—smeared the end.

The father smiled, and his teeth flared in the firelight. 'Hm,' he said. 'Precisely what I thought.'

And then, as one, all three of them looked at her. The girl tilted her head to one side as if sniffing the air for prey; the father turned his head a full one-eighty degrees, his neck cracking like the wood in the fireplace. His eyes darted with orange, saliva oozing off his lips.

The mother turned her head too, only her eyes were blank and her mouth was still frozen in that horrible scream. She almost tipped out of her chair as her body twisted, the iron stake in her chest twisting with her. Blood trickled from her nostrils, fresh and wet.

'No,' Edith shook her head. 'What do you...'

She fumbled behind her for the seam in the wall, for the door she'd come through, but it was gone.

'Please—'

The shape at the father's feet bulged, twitched, shot around the armchair, scuttling like a bug.

'Fetch,' the father whispered, his voice like ice, and the shape darted towards her.

The boy crawled like a dog, moving quick, his bald head small and round and smeared with bloody handprints. His eyes were rolled up in his head, his tongue hanging out of his mouth. Edith screamed as he pawed across the carpet towards her, slobbering madly.

His ears were stitched to his scalp and his fingers had been nailed together so that his hands were flat slabs. He could only have been four or five, but his skin was white and wrinkled. He was a demon.

Edith stumbled as the boy-dog lunged for her, swinging her pike on instinct. It smacked the boy's skull and he yipped as he was struck backwards. Edith looked behind her for an escape, for a door or a way out of here, but there was only the window—

'Darling,' the father sighed, and Edith stared in horror as the mother stood up from her chair. She moved like Edith imagined a corpse would: her legs and arms jerked and twisted as she bent up onto them and turned around, the poker in her chest wobbling as she spun. 'Kill her.'

Mother smiled. Blood bubbled out of her mouth.

'No,' the girl said, wrenching herself off the chaise lounge and stepping forward. 'She's mine.'

Something crashed to Edith's left and she looked as the boy-dog lilted up onto his feet, bounding for her again. She jabbed her pike forward and missed, grazing his shoulder. As he bounded for her shins she swung downward and heard the thick *bonk* of wood on bone as it smacked the top of his skull. Whirling around, her eyes widened as she saw Mother coming for her, moving like Death itself. Edith ducked to one side as Mother ripped the poker from her own chest and stabbed madly—blindly—in the air with it. Tumbling away from the swinging spike, Edith stumbled forward and nearly tripped over the boy-thing snapping at her heels. She rushed for the window. Father's neck went *click-click-click* as he turned his head to watch her. Raising the pike high, Edith prepared to smash the butt of the thing into the nearest windowpane—

And something curled around the pike and ripped it from her hands.

Edith turned, just in time to see something black and wet slither away from her, dragging the pike with it. Her mouth opened.

The girl stood beside the chess board, tentacles rippling from her arms and mouth. Thin, black lengths of muscle and sinew, pulsing and dripping ink. They whipped about the room, two of them curled around the pike, and Edith watched as she flung it toward the hearth. Chess pieces shattered and flew across the floor.

The girl smiled around the thin, flexing tentacle pouring out of her mouth, her lips no longer stitched together but bleeding, ripped apart.

'Oh, shit,' Edith said, looking back to the window, thrusting an elbow into the glass. It bounced off.

Outside, a row of orange pinpricks had gathered at the tree-line. Lit fires on pikes, moving forward.

They're coming...

And then a tentacle smacked her neck and coiled around it like a lasso and she was wrenched from the window and into the room.

CHAPTER ELEVEN
ESSENCES

The stairs seemed to ascend forever.

Morgan Fossey climbed into the dark, exhausted, his chest still pounding. When he had been climbing for eight or ten minutes, he heard something downstairs—Abram was calling for him—but when he rushed to the banister and looked down, the entrance hall was gone. He just saw black. Even the bottom of the stairs had been consumed by shadow. And the shadow was rising.

For a moment he stood there, watching wide-eyed as the inky black smog downstairs begun to creep over the next step, and the next, rolling toward him and *up*, and then he stopped watching and decided to run.

Taking the stairs two at a time took the wind out of him and made his leg hurt like hell, but when he looked back he saw that the wet blackness was coming faster now, washing over each step and swallowing them all with ease. He did not stop to think what might happen when the dark reached him.

The banister was splintered and rough, each step creaking with his weight. Some sagged beneath his feet and cracked; through the holes and splits in some, he saw the same darkness, as though it ran through the staircase like blood.

Looking up, still he saw that same dark, although it was retreating; perhaps this would go forever. No, he certainly couldn't last that long; it would last until the darkness beneath caught up to him. Then, *then*, the darkness above would come crashing down—

At this thought, the shadows at the top of the stairs stopped retreating and begun to form the shape of a landing. He glanced down and saw nothing but black. Three or four steps behind him, and then the rest was gone, disappeared beneath the chewing, smouldering tongues of black that whipped and darted after him. He leapt the last few, grabbed for the banister to haul himself onto the landing, spun around—

The stairs disappeared and the blackness stopped rising, shimmering right at the edge of the landing. If he wanted to get back down, he'd have to find another way.

'I'm dreaming,' he murmured, nursing his wounded leg. He had to be. Or he'd died, out there on the battlefield—more likely, he thought—and this was Hell.

Gingerly, he crawled forward, reached out to touch the black, swelling surface that had eaten away the stairs. His hands hovered above the shadow and he watched its surface writhe, almost hypnotic. Like night folded in on itself and throbbing, inches from the pads of his fingers.

He recoiled.

Better ways to die, he thought—or, in the case that he was already dead, to die a second time over—and he stood on his feet and turned to face the landing.

It was narrow, railed on one side by more banister—a quick glance over it told him that there was no way down; if he jumped, he'd fall into a pool of the same inky blackness—and on his left, a blue-papered wall.

He walked along awhile, traversing the silent corridor. One moment he thought he smelled smoke, heard the sounds of hunting; the next, he caught fragments of conversation, heard muffled screams. The wall seemed to rippled as his shadow passed across it...

Light. There had to be some somewhere, he thought, or he'd not be able to see. He paused, turning back toward the staircase.

A door, set into the wall right above the stairs. It hadn't been there before.

'What the shitting Pope Innocent is this?'

It was ajar, and through it, he saw light. A soft, steady blue light, not flickering but pulsing softly. Moonlight through clouds. Slowly, he moved back toward the door. Perhaps it had been there. He'd been scared out of his mind; he could quite easily have missed it.

'Hello?' he called, pressing his fingers to the wood. The hinges groaned as the door swung in a few inches. 'Anyone in there?'

He opened the door all the way and peered inside.

The master bedroom was wide and open, peppered with furniture that didn't fit; a huge wardrobe in one corner rattled quietly, trembling as though the wind were blowing through it. A ladder had been leant awkwardly against the far wall, and above it a trapdoor—into what Morgan presumed must be an attic—hung open. A low, squat chest of draws on his right stood beside a tall and narrow cabinet. Bluish light poured in through a small window across from him and draped the thin blankets covering a crooked bed. The frame was wrought iron, twisted into bent and broken spikes. The mattress was stuffed with straw.

Meat hung from hooks all around the ceiling.

They had been screwed there by a crude hand, and some were weighed down so heavily by the stinking carcasses hanging from them that the chains had begun to sag from the plaster, their metal brackets bending. Whatever smith had crafted the hooks had made them sharper than anything Morgan had seen; he tried not to look up, but couldn't help but cast his eyes over the thick slabs of streaky pink dangling before him. Maggots gathered in knotted holes and crawled over exposed ribs; pink coils hung loose from the hollowed-out inside of broken animal bodies.

There was a bloody apron draped over the end of the bed. Greenish, made of a shiny kind of material he'd never seen. The bedsheets, too, were made of a material that looked... wrong, somehow, thinner than they should. Almost translucent.

And on the bed itself, a leather-bound sketchbook.

Morgan hobbled forward, dipping his head beneath a swaying lamb's carcass as he reached for the book. Cautious, but curious. Drops of red scattered the face of the book. He flipped it open.

'Jesus...'

A double-page spread was covered in rabid scribblings, each word scrawled over itself a dozen times, greasy, bloody fingerprints in the corners:

> *Must be bled to be*
> *Kill*
> *Feed him*
> *Must be*
> *KILL*
> *Must be BLED*
> *KILL FEED KILL*

Morgan turned the page and swallowed, his eyes moving uneasily over a drawing of some mad kind of creature: a pig with three heads, a boar of enormous proportions, hooves bursting from bony limbs, spines rippling across its back. some kind of cursed abomination, looming over a ragged church building like a bovine god.

Morgan turned the page again.

> *The library is the only room you'll be safe.*

> —M.P.

Almost breathless, Morgan turned another

page, heart pounding as insane ramblings, scribbled over drawings of crazed animals and bloody, grinning mouths, leapt off the page at him. Turning slowly, he sat on the edge of the bed to read through the rest of the book—

And something wriggled beneath him.

Morgan leapt onto his feet, whirling round. The sheets were still. Nothing. And then...

His eyes widened as the thin, translucent sheets rippled. No... *pulsed.*

Skin, he realised. The pinkish material—blue in the moonlight filtering in through the window—was stricken through with deep, red veins, stitched together in places. Leather, but not torn from any cow's hide.

And somehow it was still alive, still had blood running through it. He watched as it throbbed again.

Groaning, he turned and wretched onto the floor, doubling over, heaving up nothing but the dust from his lungs. His throat stung.

And something grabbed his ankle.

He yelped, dropping the book, twisting his leg free of the clawed hand. Looking down, he saw the sheet had drooped over the edge of the bed, and a fleshy, pink hand had pushed through the thin material and was reaching for him, the semi-see-through fingers clutching and unclutching. The sheet twitched again and another hand pushed through it, fingers rising from bumps and stretching. He backed away, heard the rattling of the wardrobe again, looked toward it—more hands thrust from the wood, veined with the grain of it, dark and marbled and knotted like they were formed from the very oak itself. They wriggled and clawed at him and as he looked around the room he saw more, stretching out from the floorboards, from the walls. More began to warp and twist out of the glass window, the skin shimmering and the veins run through with blue clouds of moonlight. There was a clear path across the floorboards and he stumbled along it as more hands, now becoming arms, bent out of the wood with horrible creaks and moans and grabbed and swiped for him. He cried out as claws brushed his legs and batted his knees and then he was there, in the corner of the room, the only corner where the walls weren't trying to grab him, and with him, here, was—

The ladder.

He wrestled it from its place against the wall and looked up, into the attic. The house had been guiding him upward all along and now it wanted him to climb further still. A grey-skinned hand grabbed at his boot and he almost tripped kicking it away. The sound of glass splintering over and over again echoed throughout the room as the window-hands bent around to claw at his face. Hurriedly he propped the ladder into the open trapdoor in the ceiling and awkwardly began to climb.

The attic was dark, impossibly so, and he was reminded of the shadows that had chased him upstairs.

Something coughed in the corner of the room. Something weak and broken.

Below him, he could still hear the wriggling hands and the groaning of the floorboards they'd sprung from.

'Hello?' Morgan called quietly into the

dark.

'*Hell—ohh...*'

The voice was old. A woman's. An echo.

'Who are you?' Morgan asked. 'Where am I?'

'*Who... where...*'

Now the echo was mocking. Morgan opened his mouth to respond, but before he could the voice spoke again:

'*Price...*'

Morgan paused. 'Price of what?' he said.

'*Price Manor...*'

After a moment, he understood. 'Price Manor. That's where I am?'

'*Yes...*'

'And who are you?'

'*Price Manor...*'

'Yes, I know. But who—all right, it doesn't... look, what the hell is this place? What's going on here? And what are those... *things* that chased me up here?'

A shape shifted in the dark. It was bony and its eyes flared in the moonlight slipping in through a tiny, round window. '*The house... is hungry. Needs more...*'

'More?' Morgan asked, but he already knew the answer.

'*More... men. Women. Children...*'

'It's going to eat us?'

He heard the shadowy owner of the voice smile. Around him, the darkness was growing softer, gritty with shades of blue, as his eyes became accustomed to it. '*In... a way.*'

Morgan shook his head, glancing down to the trapdoor by his feet. Through it, he saw the wooden arms stretching from the floorboards curling and grabbing at the air.

'*The house will do... everything... it can. Create. Destroy. Feed.*'

'And what are you, then?' he said. 'Are you trapped here, too? I can help you... I have friends, downstairs—'

'*Not for long.*'

He shivered.

'*It will kill you all.*'

'Why?'

'*You are here.*'

Morgan stepped forward. 'Look, you—'

He saw her by the window, her head turned toward it. A bony shape wrapped in thin bedsheets. Spidery white hair crawled across her scalp. 'It will devour you,' she whispered. 'Your men will fall here.'

'No,' Morgan said. 'You're wrong. What... what are you? Why are you so sure this *place* won't fall?'

Her face twisted. He imagined she must be smiling again, but the shadows were so ingrained into the wrinkles and crevices of her features that he couldn't make them out at all. 'The house falls only if it lets you go. And it will not.'

'What does that mean? What does any of this...'

Morgan hesitated.

'I found a book,' he said. 'In the bedroom. And meat, hanging from the ceiling. Whose room was that?'

The old woman tipped her head toward him a little. 'The butcher,' she whispered. She sounded like her throat was filled with sand. 'He came here once. Or... the house came to him. Found him.'

'He's still here?'

'Yes... and no.'

'What?'

'Those who die here... stay here,' she said. Clearly, it hurt her to talk. Nonetheless, she seemed to be able to sense his fear, and she was enjoying it. 'The butcher wandered inside. Like you and your men. He had his chance to leave... and he misused it. Drawn to the spirit of this place, he chose to stay.

'Eventually, the manor grew bored with him. He is an essence, now.'

'An essence?'

'Those who die here, stay here,' she repeated, her voice stronger, clearer. 'Their essence remains. The house's to play with. He is with the spirits of this place, now.'

Morgan swallowed. 'So what killed him?'

The woman turned her head fully toward him, and he saw her face clearly for the first time. She was skeletal, withered, her bones clearly visible through patches of semi-translucent skin—the same that had been cut into squares and stretched and stitched into blankets in the master bedroom—and her eyes were jelly in deep, sunken sockets. Decay clung to her, her chest sagging and empty, her throat spindly and useless. 'The family,' she whispered. '*My* family.'

And with that, she rose from the bed and her bones cracked like rotten wood.

CHAPTER TWELVE
ADVANCING FORCES

General Oliver Abram was alone; that much was clear the moment he stepped through the door. There was nothing here with him in the darkness. There was, especially, no sign of Morgan Fossey.

He moved slowly down a stone corridor, his eyes pinned to the tiny, flickering dot of red light in the distance. Things were otherwise pitch, but if he put out both hands and moved carefully he found he could quite easily gauge the kind of space he was in; the floor beneath him was a narrow walkway of haphazard stone slabs, uneven shapes roughly jammed together, lips and cracks projected so violently upwards that he couldn't help but feel along them with the soles of his boots. The walls either side were stone, but had not been so much built as carved; it was like walking through a tunnel into a cave, and as he pressed on he found that the floor sloped down a little. After walking what must have been a good quarter-mile—impossible, he thought, in a house this size; even if he'd somehow sloped down so much that he was now *underneath* the house, surely the foundations could not have spread so far beneath the field in which they'd found the building—he turned to look back and saw that the door he'd come through had shrunk to a tiny square of soft, grey light, the hallway only visible through that little slot in the darkness. And yet, the red light he was moving toward was no closer.

Swallowing, he kept walking.

Half a mile farther, Abram found that he had to keep his arms pressed to his sides to squeeze through the tunnel. Narrower here, and shorter too, he thought, although he still could not see bugger all.

The red light had swelled a little, although

it was still just a dot at the very farthest point of his field of view. He kept moving.

By the time Abram reached the door, the tunnel around him was tight enough that he had to bend his body forward, that he could hardly breathe for an odd change in the air pressure; and yet he'd been compelled to walk for what must have been a mile and a half—or two, even—when he should have turned around at any point to head back to his men. He looked back now, and saw that the door at the end of the tunnel had become a tiny dot of white, almost wholly invisible. Still, at least it was open. Despite the unlikely straightness of the tunnel, he fancied he'd have a difficult time walking back without that light to guide him.

He turned back to the door.

It was huge, filling the space entirely. The rock walls opened up a little right here at the end of the tunnel, and the door must have been a good nine feet tall, at least six or seven wide. Solid oak, the kind of wood ships were made of. Heavy iron plates strapped it to thick hinges and a black, salt-encrusted knob was set into the very centre of the door.

Stepping back again, Abram peered through a keyhole in the door. Red light flared through it, bright as the sun—blinding, in fact.

Cold air wept through the keyhole and he shivered. Gently, he laid a hand on the knob. Octagonal, the edges sharp and gritty. He turned it and something *click*ed.

The door opened and red light flooded the tunnel.

'Holy hell...'

Candles at every edge and corner of the room, some mounted to the walls on iron brackets, some standing free of any support, wax dripping down their narrow limbs to fuse them to wooden and stone surfaces. The light from these candles was not orange or blue but a deep, blood red; the room seemed to bleed even as it burned.

He stepped forward, eyes adjusting to the wallowing, fluid light, and found himself in a chapel. The room was almost as large as the nave of a church, but the only window was right at the end of the room behind an enormous, stone altar; a thin, tall window that looked out onto the forest and fields. No stained glass, no paintings on any of the walls. The stone was largely unmarked, although long, irregular scratches had rent the lime in places. Claw marks.

Abram pushed forward between two rows of long, polished pews, running a hand over the dark wood as he passed. The aisle was long and he must have passed two dozen pews on either side, but there was no sign of a Bible or prayer sheet anywhere. His eyes were fixed on the altar, on the abomination carved in stone before him.

The stone-faced figure was almost that of a crucified man, but where his arms were splayed out they became the tentacles of some undersea creature, whirling and spiralling back to coil around his body. His face had been clawed and ripped away; the tusks that thrust out from the rock behind him and through his hips were those of a giant pig. A wooden cross was tipped on the faceless man's back, as if he'd been carrying it; it must have been knocked or broken at some point, for it was upside-down.

Abram stood before the altar and drew in a deep breath. The cold in the chapel was unbearable, the red light unhinged and mad, but he felt compelled to stay. Clearly, this place had not been built for him, but now he felt it was exactly what he needed.

He crumpled to his knees, hitting the stone floor hard.

For a long time he knelt in silence, his eyes on the ground, and then he began to speak.

'God, if you're...

'Or, if you're *not*...

'Anyway...'

He took another breath, looked up. Started again, his eyes on the mutilated face of the abomination propping up the altar.

'God, I hope you can forgive me. Forgive us. I have never... never prayed enough, never believed enough, though I know that isn't particularly uncommon.'

He paused. Wind rippled through the room, disturbing red swathes of light. The orange whiskers of his beard trembled. He continued.

'But this war... one that has gone on for far too long already... I hope you can forgive all I've done. Please, know that I repent. That I regret it all. The things Cromwell has had us do... all for glory, for victory, for what is *right*, I know that, but...

'Christ, the things he has had us do...'

He looked around, looked behind him. He had the uncanny feeling that he was being watched, that he wasn't alone after all in here. But he saw nobody.

'I hope to undo it all,' he said quietly. 'Our mission... it is not one given us by Cromwell. My men, they believe these are orders from on high, but this mission—our last—that's on me. My choice. My decision. And if it goes wrong—any more wrong than it has already, I should say—then I hope you'll spare them.'

He looked down, toward the tusks that pierced the statuesque figure's hips, and saw that thin trails of alabaster-white ran down the stone, down his legs. Where the granite had once been polished. By water, running from the wounds? By... something else?

'Whatever punishment for my intentions, let it come unto me,' Abram whispered. 'Let the rest go. This mission... I can't do it alone, I need them. But I can't have you take them for what they've done, not when it was all for me.

'Whatever's coming, let it come to me. If I am to lie there bleeding while the others go free, then so be it.

'But please, God, or... whoever... please let us be successful. Don't let my Nowhere Boys down.'

He stood.

'Amen, or whatever.'

For a long time, silence. The red light waned, and his eyes moved to the window behind the altar, to the greys and greens of the world outside.

Then something in the air changed.

A scraping sound behind him. Deafening, all at once filling the room, the long, low groan of wood on stone; he snapped his head round to look and saw the pews moving, saw them shifting.

'No,' he said, stumbling away from the altar as rows of wooden benches turned and scraped themselves across the stone-slat floor, crashing into each other, forming right angles. The sound of creaking, cracking wood joined the sound of scraping and he clamped his hands over his ears as the pews began to stretch, lengthening, becoming walls. Their backs were wrenched up, became first waist-height then chest-height, and by the time he realised what was happening he was too late.

He backed away, shaking his head as silence fell across the chapel. The room seemed significantly smaller now.

Between him and the door, the pews had formed a maze. A labyrinth of gilded wooden walls, taller than he was. Two pews nearest to him had stretched all the way out to the walls on either side, and almost to the ceiling, so that the only way into the maze was a narrow opening between them directly in front of him.

'Oh, shit,' he whispered, backing up and hitting the altar. The spikes of the tusks prodded the small of his back. He winced, turning his head:

No way out. The window, even if he could

smash the glass, was too narrow for anyone to fit through, and he had no means of breaking away the stone around the frame.

The window...

'Oh, Christ...' he murmured.

Figures at the edge of the forest, figures in Cavalier uniform. Almost silhouettes, but he saw blood, saw smoke. The retreated forces that Morgan had warned them about. They had gone into the woods to regroup, and that done, they had decided to converge, to attack the house...

They were coming.

He had to warn the others.

'Oh, bollocks,' he said, turning back to the wooden-walled maze before him. Red lights clawed at his back as he dived in.

CHAPTER THIRTEEN
MR. WRITER

Michael tumbled from the rope and it screamed through his hand, carving a thick, raw strip out of his palm. He turned almost immediately as he hit the floor, thrusting into the dark with his knife.

The serrated forward nicked something hard with a *click* and he saw the flashing of teeth as one of the awful little creatures came for him, bleeding from its gums. He twisted his wrist and swiped to the left, jamming the knife with a meaty *shhnk* into the thing's skull. It slid easily through thin plates of bone and found something wet and squishy. The creature's eyes rolled up and filled with blood. Michael kicked it off his knife and a jet of thick black spurted into the air as he pulled the blade free.

Then another was on him. He could feel a third raking claws across his back, digging through the material of his uniform, and he whirled around, kicking out wildly as he jabbed and slashed with the knife. Another came from above, dropping from the ceiling and onto his head, scuttling around to the back of his neck and opening its mouth wide to take a bite—

Michael stumbled back, slamming into the nearest pillar. There was a sick, wet *crunch* as the thing on his neck was squashed against the concrete. It fell limply from him but already another had leapt onto his chest; he stabbed awkwardly at its back and, as if sensing the knife coming at it from behind, the creature dived onto the dusty floor. Michael's eyes went wide as he stopped himself—stopped the blade—two inches from his own flesh. Immediately he swung it forward again, ripping a gunky black gash across the belly of another creature. Another gnawed at his leg; its teeth had come through the material of his trousers now and he could feel it nibbling at his shin. He kicked out, bringing the knife down simultaneously, and as the clinging creature flew upward he drove the blade into its shoulder and levered it forward. The creature shrieked as its arm fell limp, attached to its shoulder only by a thin, black string of sinew. Blood splashed the floor and Michael's boots.

'Jesus,' he panted, backing against the pillar and casting his eyes across the room. More were coming. The shadows crawled with them. He could hear them skittering across the ceiling, and when he looked up he saw that the dark above was alive with them, a mass of them. Gristly skin glistened wetly in the half-light, dead eyes glinting.

His gaze froze on a thin, wooden door across the room. Between it and him, dozens of the creatures. Hundreds, all converging hungrily on him.

Michael lurched forward, swinging his fist into the brittle jaw of a demonic, rat-headed thing as it flew toward his face. His knuckles connected. Something shattered. He kicked another out of the way and stomped down hard on a third's skull. Another *crunch*.

He staggered through more of them—clinging to his arms and legs, now, too many—and yelped as one of them tore a chunk out of his left forearm. Heading for another pillar, he swung the injured arm and smashed the creature's rump against the concrete. Losing the grip in its legs, it fell, a hunk of bloody flesh still in its mouth. Broken on the floor, it chewed contentedly as though the use of its legs had never been that big a deal.

Bursting from pillar to pillar, Michael stabbed and kicked and ducked beneath the attacks of leaping creatures as they lunged for his eyes. They were starting to drop from the ceiling now and crawl down the pillars toward him, and the door was still so far away...

Warmth splashed his face as something ripped a part of his ear away. He screamed, thrusting up a blind elbow and catching the creature in its gut. No time to curse the pain. He pushed on to the next pillar, ramming his side—and two creatures attached like leeches to his arm—into the hard surface. They howled and fell away. Carving another's neck wide open with his knife he practically rolled to the next pillar, stumbling to his feet as another came for his throat—

'Fuck *off*!' he yelled, thrusting his head forward and butting the thing in the skull. It crumpled, falling to the ground, and he stood over it and brought a boot crashing down, crushing its spindly throat.

The door. Closer now. He pushed forward, biting and kicking as a horde of the things came at him. He kicked out and felt something heavy resist his boot momentarily before swaying and toppling to the floor. The shattering of dozens of bottles filled the room like a million piercing, glass-throated screams, and the sour smell of decades-old wine pushed into his nostrils, musty and awful. The creatures, temporarily distracted, swarmed the fallen wine rack, giggling like schoolchildren as they splashed through puddles of slick, blood red and smashed their own skins open on the glass shards littering the ground.

Michael took his opportunity and darted forward, gaining a dozen feet or so before they realised he was still there. He grunted in pain, reaching for the doorhandle—

And a creature dropped from the ceiling and landed on his arm, bringing it down and tearing a hunk out of his wrist in the process. He screamed and thrust the knife across his body, nicking his own arm but plunging the blade deep into the creature's chin. Is eyes widened and he saw the point of the blade come up bloody through its slithering tongue and into the roof of its mouth. He pulled back and it fell away, and he reached again for the handle.

The door opened and he fell through, slamming his back against it as hundreds of tiny fists and feet crashed frantically against the wood, clawing for him. Quickly he slid a narrow, silver bolt across and staggered back, watching as the doorframe shuddered. The creatures smacked and pounded on the door and it trembled, looking as though it might split open. Looking around desperately, Michael saw that he was in a small study, hardly the size of a bathroom but filled with cabinets—cabinets made of metal, and with drawers all the way up—and he grabbed one and dragged it to the door, pressing it up against a splintered panel on the left and going for another.

As he did, the scratching and pounding stopped. As if they'd forgotten about him, or given up on him.

He stood frozen for a minute, listening. But the creatures were gone.

Breathing a sigh of relief, Michael turned to the room.

His blood froze.

A small desk in the middle of the room was littered with parchment and instruments. Slim, functional writing tools of a kind he'd never seen before. The walls erupted with bookshelves, filled to bursting with files and folders and leatherbound novels.

On the desk was a machine. A brittle husk of iron that had once been a pale shade of green, but now was the colour of vomit and spattered with patches of brown-red rust. Wheels and rotors decorated the top of the odd thing. Its face was punctuated with rows of buttons, like those on his coat, but each one was printed with a letter or symbol. A roll of yellowed paper spewed out of the mouth of the machine.

Sitting at the machine was a dead man.

Michael swallowed, moving gingerly toward the corpse in the desk chair. It looked like it had been a young man at one point, but now it was hardly recognisable. A red shirt, drawn through with crisscrossing black lines, hung off the bones of a sunken chest, greasy rags that had fallen loose as the body's flesh rotted away. The grey bones were sticky and oozed red in places. He could see the shrivelled mess of a heart inside a dusty ribcage, clinging to a collection of equally-wizened organs he couldn't name. The corpse's skull was tipped to one side, its wide, eyeless eyes massive with fear. There was a bottlecap between the skull's teeth.

Its hands were laid across the keys of the strange machine, as if it had been constructing some foul magic with it right up until the moment it had died. It stunk of decay. Blood splashed the buttons. There were no flies in the room, although Michael spied clusters of them—dead—across the desk.

Circling the desk, Michael looked at the machine over the rotten body's sunken shoulder. An eerie sense of stillness rippled through him. The paper that had crawled halfway from the cruel jaws of the machine was covered in symbols—letters. Words.

He frowned, reaching forward. He hadn't been able to read, until he'd met General Oliver Abram. But the red-haired man had insisted that they all learn, and had taught him well. This was no spell or cryptic message from the machine itself. It was a note.

Michael's gaze moved across the papers on the table. Some were stacked neatly; a bundle of a hundred pages or so caught his eye. On the first, a title:

The Family
by Nick Harper

He swallowed as he noted the ribbon of blood across the page. Part of a wider, ragged splash that covered half the table. Turning his eyes back to the strange machine, he ripped the paper from it and began to read.

It came to me once, and I refused to go in.

The house. I think it can appear wherever—whenever, perhaps—it likes. I know this because, after I ignored its call—the call of an open door—it disappeared.

It reappeared days later. Around me. I was walking through the woods when it came for me a second time. I suppose it didn't want to offer me a choice this time. It caught me. One moment I was in a forest clearing; the next, I was standing in the library.

If I'd known that was the only safe room in the house, I'd have stayed there.

A thin, bony man appeared to me in what I'd describe as a hexagonal room, a room with a grand staircase up and a great glass ceiling above. The glass was smashed. There was blood everywhere.

He told me about the house. What it does. What it needs.

And he said, "Every now and then, the imagination of this place runs a little stale." When I asked who this man was, he would not answer. But when the house—its pipes and funnels, its brickwork and boards—seemed to crack or groan, he seemed to take a breath. As though they were one and the same. He told me what the house can do. How it can manipulate shapes, create creatures, spirits, from nothing, or from memories...

He said that it had been a long time. That the house wanted something new. Something exciting, something to really make its "visitors" afraid.

And it asked me to write.

Michael glanced again at the bloodstained papers the other side of the desk. *The Family, by Nick Harper.* A story?

I wrote. The house gave me this room, left me alone. And I returned the favour by writing the best story I'd ever written. A tale of monsters, disguised as a family. The boy. The girl. The parents.

The grandmother.

The house—or the man whom I believe acted as some kind of conduit, or disguise, for it—told me that it would let me live. But when I saw what I'd created... what the house had created from my imagination...

Well, you can see what I chose to do.

Michael swallowed, stepping back from the corpse.

Make no mistake, the house had no need of me. It can conjure up demons and monsters of its own. It just wanted to play with me. To taunt me, to see how far it could push me. And it won. I can't do this anymore. The bony man has said that if I can keep writing stories for this place, it will let me go. Eventually. But now I know what it will do with these stories.

I have seen The Family kill, and I know that they will kill many more. And they are not the only monsters in this place; far from it.

This is my only way out.

Find the library. They can't reach you there. The Family, that is. Everything else that calls this place home?

Well, I suppose you'll find out.

Consider these my last words, and please... get the Christ-crapping shit out of this place.

Nick Harper
20th October 2021

Michael Caldwell took one last look at the note and let it fall from his hand and flutter to the dusty floor of the study.

Stumbling back from the corpse in the chair, he ran a hand through his hair and, with the other, gripped his bloody knife a little tighter than before.

CHAPTER FOURTEEN
THE MAZE

Red light flooded the wooden-walled maze as Abram tumbled madly through it, cold air biting at his back as he ripped through the shadows. The groans and screams of the stretching, peeling pews followed him as their backs rose to the ceiling, and there were footsteps. Everywhere, there were footsteps: the echoes of his own? Or those of something else, following him?

He tore to the right, curling around a corner and immediately left around another. The pews were still moving, still thrusting into and retreating from the centre of the room, the maze ever-changing. But he knew he was heading the right way—the way he'd come. He *had* to be.

Abram panted, paused for breath at an

intersection, narrow paths leading away from him in four directions. He turned to look behind him. Through the slim gap he'd come through, he saw light. Not the swaying red glow of the chapel but the bright, grey shade of the entrance hall. His eyes widened. 'Damn it,' he cursed, lurching towards the gap—

It closed. Two pews shunted together, slammed into each other and shut out the light.

'No!' Abram screamed, slamming his fists against the wood. He wheeled around, eyes passing over the three remaining pathways. The last—the one to his right—was now lit with that same grey glow. He pushed towards it, dread filling his stomach.

Just as he reached the tunnel, it closed. The pew to his right slid across the gap as if shoved, closing it before he could even push a hand through the opening.

'Damn you!'

He turned. Of the two openings left, one was lit with that same bright, welcoming grey.

He ran through the other.

The maze seemed to grow more complex,

more devastatingly *huge* as he moved deeper into its confines; the room had never been half as big as this, he thought, or even a fraction of the size, and yet he felt he had run through the twisting, bending corridors for days on end.

A sharp left turn sent him crashing into a dead end. The wall before him was tall and impassable and the deep, black shadows of the ceiling spilled down it in ribbons, oozing like blood. He turned back and ploughed through to the right, turning, corner after corner, turning, legs aching and tired, *turning...*

Peeling into a short, dark tunnel, he froze.

At the end of the alleyway, standing with its back to him in the shade of the impossibly tall walls on every side, was a monster. It was twice the height of a man and its frame was thin and spindly. Long, pale arms dangled below its knees, claws curled limply and drooling something thick and wet. Its pinkish skin was run through with veins that pulsed and throbbed; its entire body was coated in a viscous slick of translucent mucus.

Slowly, it turned its head and grinned at

him.

Abram backed up, eyes wide, fumbling with the walls on either side until—

His right hand plunged through an opening and he took his chance, following through with his body and running into the alleyway. He didn't turn to look back and see if the beast was following; he just ran and kept running.

Winding around a heavily canted pew, he found himself ducking beneath it—it leaned into the aisle and halved the height of his walkway. Squeezing out the other side, he turned right—

Another of the pale-skinned abominations stood before him. This time it was already turned towards him, its awful maw open and smiling. It had no eyes, he saw, but shallow pits in its face reflected a hunger that dribbled down its chin and mangled throat.

It started to move towards him and he looked round frantically, found that an alleyway to his left opened up wide, the pews drifting away to either side. He darted into the alley, ducking beneath the wide, raking claws of the creature with a yelp. 'Away, beast!' he yelled as he stumbled forward and broke into a run. An opening to his right; he took it.

Stairs, leading down. He hesitated.

Heavy, wet breathing behind him; Abram stopped hesitating and moved awkwardly down the stairs.

Bursting into a wide, round chamber, he whirled around to see twelve open doors, set equidistantly around the room. He turned to look up the stairs, and a thick slab of wood that he recognised as the warped, dark back of a pew slammed down from the ceiling and crashed into the floor, blocking the way back up.

Abram swore and glanced through the nearest door. Nothing but darkness. The same through most of them, he noticed, stepping forward cautiously. In fact, through all twelve doors, there seemed to be nothing but shadow. Except...

He moved slowly toward a door on his right, raising a hand to feel the air. A draft; no, a breeze. 'Where am I?' he whispered into the flaccid spirals of wind that funnelled out of the tunnel. 'Where do you want me to go?'

The door slammed in his face with a *bang!* that echoed through the chamber. He stumbled back and felt a breeze to his left. Turning his head, he watched as a shadow flitted across another of the doors. Moments later, it slammed shut.

'I know this game,' he murmured, a little louder. 'You think you can fool me twice?'

One by one, the doors slammed shut. He stood stoically in the middle of the chamber, waiting for the eleventh *crash!*, for the sound that would tell him only one door had been left open, that would tell him which way the wretched house wanted him to go.

Bang! Nine.

Bang! Ten.

Bang! Eleven.

He paused, swallowing hard, prepared himself to turn and face the last door, the last option—

Bang!

His blood ran cold. Casting his eyes in a wide circle, he saw that all twelve doors had closed. His options were...

Something brushed his shoulder.

Abram jumped, looking up.

A rope dangled from a hole in the ceiling. Thick, tarred threads woven together into a swinging, frayed noose.

'Oh, sh...'

He never finished. Instead, he followed the rope up, up, up—not to the ceiling, but *through* it, through a ragged hole that had appeared there.

He saw the floor of a dusty, amber-lit cellar, way above him. Saw creatures scuttling across that floor, tiny familiars drenched in shadow. How did they not fall? How could they move across that earthen surface above him without plummeting to the ground, or through the hole and into the chamber with him?

He blinked as he saw Michael Caldwell stagger across the ceiling, swiping and slashing at the creatures. 'Shuck!' Abram yelled, reaching up, grabbing for the rope—

As soon as he tugged on the coil of the noose, it snapped upwards, whipping away from him, and, as though some unholy cog had been turned, the room flipped upside down.

Abram yelled as he was flung back toward the wall. The door directly behind him opened—they all did, simultaneously, and through others he saw vast, flaming shapes, glaring white eyes in the dark—and he fell through onto his back. He landed with a *thud* and cried out again as pain rippled through him.

Scrambling to his feet, the general ran a hand through his red hair, now streaked with soot and dust, and looked around. He was back in the maze—somehow, inexplicably *back* there—and he had three options.

Behind him, a dark tunnel led… somewhere.

To his right, another opening seemed to peel away and around a corner.

Before him, a tall, pale-skinned beast, dripping with mucus and blood, breathed shallow breaths, its whole body shivering with each one.

'I know *your* game, soldier,' he said quietly, stepping forward. 'You're meant to scare me, correct? To force me away? To push me in a certain direction?'

The beast's mouth opened wide. Rows and rows of pointed teeth flared in the soft, red light of the maze.

'Well, I'm not playing,' Abram said. Slowly, he stepped back.

The creature stepped forward, mirroring his movements. Long, heavy hands hung at its sides.

Abram took another step; the creature followed.

'That's it,' he whispered, 'just a little further...'

One more step. The creature shadowed him, moved forward—

And Abram darted forward, barrelling straight for the thing's waist. It swiped with a long, pale arm and he ducked beneath it, peeling to the right—and through the opening that the creature had aligned itself with rather perfectly. As it spun around, raking the air with both sets of claws as it swiped madly at his face, Abram slid back into the tunnel—behind it, now—and ploughed forwards, down the path the thing had been guarding.

He felt a rush of air behind him and dipped his head down; claws scraped through the air where it had been and something caught in his hair, yanking a clump from the flesh of his scalp. Yelping, he wheeled around a left turn and came to a junction; one alley to the left, and one to the right.

On his left, there was fire. The end of the tunnel was ablaze with orange curls, tongues licking the wooden walls. He could feel the heat from here, felt it course towards him, claw at him...

On his right, he smelled freshly baked bread. Aunt Ophelia's freshly baked bread. He remembered the summer he'd been made to stay with her; oh, how he'd hated that house at first, but he'd come to love her as he did his own mother, come to love her baking and the endless goodies she'd stoved over...

'A worthless trick,' he said quietly, and he dived to his left and into the flames consuming the corridor.

Edith screamed as the family descended on her, a mass of slithering tentacles and tongues. She thrust a knee forward and it connected with the mouth of the lunging, biting dog-like boy attacking her shins, sending him flying back. Immediately he scuttled forward again on all fours, gnashing his teeth, his stitched-up features flashing with a kind of animalistic hunger.

'Daddy!' the daughter whined, twisting her arm and whipping a thin, black tendril around Edith's throat. It snapped loudly as it smacked her flesh and Edith gasped as it tightened. 'She's not playing fair!'

'Nicely, children...' the father said quietly, turning his head to look in Edith's direction. His eyes were ablaze with firelight, reflecting all the anger and fury of the hearth, but he was smiling. His sadistic expression was thin and bony and Edith couldn't help but stare in his direction as he stood up straight, brushing down his clothes with long, skeletal fingers. His gaze shifted to something by the fireplace, and she followed. Saw her pike lying on the carpet, stained with blood and surrounded by scattered chess pieces.

Father stepped forward, bent down, reached to pick up the pike—

'No!' Edith choked, but all the air in her lungs was gone. She could feel her skin tightening. Her eyes fell onto the fireplace and she saw something moving in the flames, something beastly and screaming and thrashing towards her—

Something shambled up to her on her right and she turned her head as best she could, swinging both fists madly. The girl's mother shuffled up, arms hanging limp, mouth open in a silent scream. The corners turned—now the scream was a smile, an awful, terrified smile—and the woman-thing's eyes flared with a bright, snaring hunger as she bent forward to plunge her teeth into Edith's neck—

Edith yanked her whole body down suddenly, pulling the tentacle down with her. Grabbing it with both hands, she twisted; the daughter shrieked with pain and the oily tendril retreated into the firelight shadows.

Edith stumbled back to the wall as Mother turned on her, eyes rolling madly. The dog-boy was at her feet again and she kicked out—it caught her foot in its mouth and bit—she yelped, shaking him off, rolling onto her back, and now Father was standing above her, the pike in his hand, and she saw deep, black wells open up in his eyes as he smiled down at her and raised the pike above his head and thrust the ragged, splintered point of it down toward her chest—

'Christ!' Edith yelled, rolling to one side. She saw Daughter standing to her left, tentacles jetting out from every part of her body like spurts of blood, coiling and tightening and stretching around the room. Her hair flew madly as if she was standing in the wind; her eyes were the same hollow black as her father's.

Edith felt niggling at her leg and slammed her thighs together, crushing the dog-boy's head and sending him wriggling backwards, shaking his skull madly as if trying to loose himself of fleas.

'Fuck off!' she yelled. 'All of you, fuck off!'

Mother's hands dug into her armpits and yanked her to her feet, pinning her against the wall. A wet, black tentacle thrashed across her face and she winced at the *smack* and the bright, warm shot of pain at her cheek.

Father stood before her, the sharp tip of the pike aimed at her eyeball.

But she wasn't looking at him. She was looking past him, at the fireplace. There was something *in* there. She saw its howling face, claws scratching at the hearth, digging its way out of the flames. One of them? Another horrific family member, come to burn her?

The dog-boy was on her chest suddenly, crawling over her, and Edith cried out in agony as it clamped its teeth around her shoulder and ripped a chunk of flesh away. Blood splashed Father's face and he smiled, jabbing the pike forward.

Edith ducked her head and the spear missed the top of her skull by inches. Mother grabbed her by the arms and yanked her away from the wall, her silent-screaming face suddenly alive with bright red anger, biting and clawing; Edith sent a fist into the woman-thing's throat and staggered back. Tentacles thrashed forward and whipped around her body, constraining her, one curling around her chin and tilting back her head as Father came at her with the pike again—

And then a pair of smouldering, grey hands appeared around Father's neck and squeezed, pulling the deranged bastard back into the firelight. 'Get down!' a voice yelled, and Edith scrambled back, into the grip of the tentacles, crumpling to her knees as something slammed Father into the wall. Father gasped loudly as his skull splintered; the thing with the burnt hands plunged a thumb into his eye and it burst in an explosion of oily black jelly. Slamming his head into the wall again, the thing laughed bitterly, and Edith saw a familiar face.

Grinning, she thrust up her good arm and grabbed the nearest tendril, pulling herself to her feet and spinning round to face the daughter. She yanked, hard, and came face-to-face with the young abomination. 'How did you get here?' she yelled as she sent her forehead flying into the girl's face. The daughter faltered, tentacles whipping back. Edith floundered, grabbing at the discarded chess board laying at her feet, and swung it madly.

The board shattered across Daughter's black-eyed face and the girl screamed. Edith whirled around to see Abram struggling against Mother's grabbing hands as Father drove the spear at his waist. 'Couldn't let you—die here...' he managed, swinging an elbow into Father's nose. Blood came down the monstrous man's face in a wall of slick, shining red. Abram roared, turning on him, all fists and vigour, and Edith saw that his face was horribly burned, raw blisters bubbling wetly across his left cheek. He was covered in soot, his clothes ruined and black, his eyes red and bulging. 'I need you—Edith—'

'I can see that,' Edith murmured, diving forward and wrenching the dog-boy from Abram' knees. She flung it into the wall and scrambled back as it scuttled toward her again. 'Jesus, what are these things?'

Abram fell, crumpling to the floor. 'Edith— we need to make it out—of here... the mission—'

'Fuck your mission!' Edith yelled suddenly, twisting her body out of the reach of a thrashing tentacle. 'Do you really think killing that bastard—'

'All right'—Abram' head flew back as Father's hands dug into his burned hair and yanked him toward the fire—'let's just try and not *die* before the Cavaliers arrive!'

Edith's blood froze in her body. She grabbed Daughter's hair and yanked, slamming her head into her brother's. There was a sick, wet *crunch* and something tore wetly in her ruined shoulder. 'How many?' she yelled.

'More than we thought—more than Morgan thought—sixty, maybe, seventy—'

All at once, everything stopped.

A full second passed before Edith realised the dog-boy had stopped gnawing at the air around her. She whirled around and saw Mother move back, shambling into the shadows, her screaming mouth opening wider as her head fell back, limp.

Behind her, Daughter's tentacles retreated

into her body.

Father lay on the carpet, panting, the pike lying beside him.

'What's...'

Abram blinked, looking first at Edith then at each family member as they began to retreat, to remove themselves and move back to their places around the broken chess table. Father sat in the armchair he'd been in when Edith had entered the living room, sinking gently into the leather and staring straight ahead as though he'd never moved. His face was splashed with blood.

Mother sat across from him, beckoning for their daughter to join her on her lap. The dog-boy curled up at her feet. For a moment they just sat there.

'Why have they stopped?' Abram panted. 'You, there'—he directed his call to the daughter—'what is this?'

Daughter blinked. They all did, the four of them, all at once, four sets of black eyes snapping shut for a fraction of a second. And then, as one, they turned their heads toward the far side of the room. Mother's cracked as she turned to look a full one-eighty degrees behind her.

Edith nursed her wounded shoulder, wincing as she bent down to pick up her discarded pike. Her eyes lifted to the end of the room, and she saw it. A door that she hadn't noticed before, nestled between two low-hanging velvet curtains. No, it hadn't *been* there before, she was sure of it.

But now it was.

A sign above the door, in an elaborate golden legend, read *Library*.

CHAPTER FIFTEEN
THE LIBRARY

Michael Caldwell whirled around as a solid, heady *crunch* split through the study door. The splintering sound echoed around the little room and he saw that the frame had begun to tremble; the creatures had not been retreating, he supposed, but regrouping, and now they were attacking in force.

A hinge buckled.

Michael swallowed, backing up and crashing into the desk behind him. A sharp pain shot up his thighs and jolted up through his spine. He wiped a slick of blood off the blade of his knife and brandished it, facing the shuddering door as things the other side kicked and crashed against it.

No way out. He glanced furtively around the room, refusing to look for more than a second in the direction of the ghoulish corpse in the desk chair. Nothing. No doors, no windows—had there been one, before, or had he imagined that?—no god-fucking-damn way out.

Another *crunch* and he wheeled back around, eyes widening as the wood cracked open, right down the middle of the door. The handle spun and screamed as the frame punched out from the wall, little by little—

Crack.

Michael staggered back, scrambling behind the desk as the door bent open and a whirlwind of demons thrashed into the room, crawling and writing over each other in a mad storm of grey skin and beady eyes. The smell of death followed them and he balked, raising the knife in front of his face as he backed into the corner of the room.

A sharp corner rammed his shin and he yelped in surprise, sidestepping the thing and looking down:

A glass cabinet. The same glass cabinet that he'd seen in the entrance hall—or certainly thought he'd seen, at least—except now it was bloody and scratched, as though it had lived through twice as many wars as he had.

And something glinting inside, through the glass, beckoning him...

Michael ducked beneath a swinging claw and thrust the handle of the knife into the glass pane that made up the door of the cabinet. The glass shattered loudly, sprinkling the inside of the little wooden thing; he fumbled for the shelf at the back of the cabinet, grabbing at the dully shining object inside—

A key. He wrenched it free and turned as a creature raked its claws across his chest. His uniform tore and blood pooled. The sharp, stinging pain sent him reeling into a corner of the room. He stabbed upwards with the knife, barely pausing to look at the key in his other hand—he could feel it, though, thick and rusted and clunky—as a shower of black blood rained down on him. The biting, clawing familiars filled the room, swarming over him, and through a haze of scratching claws and bony elbows he saw it.

The door. The door he'd come through had

changed. It had reformed, rebuilt itself somehow, no longer lying in shattered splinters but in its frame, solid—and different. The wood was marbled and varnished so well that it shone, and the handle was a polished brass.

Emblazoned across two wooden panels was the word *Library*.

Safety. *Find the library*, the dead writer's note had read. *They can't find you there...*

And now it was being presented to him.

Another trick?

'Doesn't matter,' he growled, and he ploughed forward into the wriggling mass of creatures. He felt bone crack open as he stamped on a small skull, felt digging claws pierce the flesh of his thighs as they crawled up his body, leapt onto him. But the sight of the exit had renewed his vigour and he pushed through, slashing throats and limbs with the serrated blade as he bent his elbows out and punched them into wide, gnarly maws. He was yelling, he realised, screaming as he fought his way through, and then he thrust his arm up and jammed the head of the key into a creature's eyeball. It burst and sprayed cool jelly over his face.

He reached the door, fumbled with the handle as demons clawed at his hands and arms—*god-damn handle won't turn*—kicking out as more attached themselves to his legs, and then he was on his knees, crumpled, useless, still scrambling desperately for the door—*use the fucking key!*—as more yanked at his hair, chewing at his shoulders and neck. They were up to his chin now, burying him, climbing and clambering over him, and his arm slipped and fell away and he knew he was dead, finally, fucking properly dead—

And then something warm and wet splashed him from above and he groaned, peeling his head back as a creature tugged with sharp claws at his eyelid. He looked up.

The skeleton of the writer stood above him, clutching the machine from the desk in both hands. The keys were covered with blood and a wide swathe of red coiled around one bulky, metal corner. As Michael watched the dead man swung, lifeless skull spattered with blood, bringing the writing machine crashing through a squirming ribbon of creatures and sending them flying.

The skeleton opened its grinning mouth. Finally, the bottlecap that had been lodged there fell loose.

'Go,' it whispered, its voice the voice of death.

Michael plunged his arm upward and slammed the key into the lock of the door and twisted.

The door fell open and he collapsed through it, glancing back one more time as the demons crawled over their new target, chewing scraps of decayed flesh off of Nick Harper's bones as he sunk beneath them.

Michael let the door close and fell to his knees.

'Christ, look at the state of you,' came a voice from behind him.

Michael shook his head, blood oozing from scratches and pockmarks in his flesh. His left eye was bruised so badly it was almost closed; his fingers were still curled tightly around the knife handle, but they shook. 'Please,' he moaned, 'please, no more...'

'Shuck,' came the voice again. A woman's voice. 'Shuck, it's me. It's us.'

'Please...' Michael whispered, shoulders sagging. 'I can't. Enough of your trickery, demon.'

'Hey,' Edith said, grabbing his shoulder and bending down into his field of view. 'Less of the "demon", all right?'

Michael blinked. Slowly, he stood, trembling on his feet.

'Welcome back, friend,' the general said behind him. He turned.

'Abram?'

Abram nodded. His skin was burned horribly, his own eyes rheumy and wet. His hair had turned a dreadful, sooty grey.

Beside him, Edith rubbed his arm. 'They got to you, too?' she said. Her shoulder was crudely bandaged with a scrap of cloth. She looked beaten beyond hell. 'The family?'

The family...

'What the hell is this place?' Michael murmured.

'I'd love to know,' said Morgan, standing across the room from him. 'I think we all would.'

For the first time, Michael took note of the room he'd fallen into. The library. The walls were stacked impossibly high with books, spines printed with red and gold. Ornate furniture scattered the edges of the room and deep, lush curtains fell bloody and breathless down the walls. Against a wide, oaken desk, a painting or mirror had been covered in a thick cloth. The cloth rippled softly, as if a draft were carried against it.

'What the fuck is this room, let alone anything else?'

'I don't know,' Abram said, 'but I think we're safe here.'

Michael counted. Shook his head. He, Edith, Abram and Morgan. Four of them had made it. 'Not all of us...' he said.

'The kid.' Morgan's eyes widened.

Michael turned to Edith. 'I'm sorry,' he said, 'I shouldn't have—'

She shook her head.

'Is he...?'

'I don't know,' she said. 'But wherever he is, I'd say it's a safe bet he's in danger.'

CHAPTER SIXTEEN
THE BUTCHER'S TABLE (III)

The cleaver came down.

Waves of panic rippled through Charlie's body at once, dark spots dancing and swelling at the corners of his vision. His chest pounded; he was disoriented, lost, and—

this is now

—the cleaver came *down*.

He screamed as pain blistered his hand. The blade cleaved through bone and sprayed warmth across his body. Three of the fingers on his right hand disappeared, severed instantly, tumbling to the floor, and rivers of pain shot up into his hand and down, sloppily, onto the floor. 'Fuck!' he yelled, thrashing his whole body on the table as the cleaver withdrew, bloody. 'Fuck, fucking—*shitting*—fuck!'

The cleaver came down again, screaming towards his eyes. Charlie bucked, snapping his neck forward; with a *shunk!* the blade buried itself in the table and he kicked and thrashed madly, yanking his arm. He screamed again as the leather strap around his wrist slid over the bloody, wet nubs of his knuckles, dragging across the exposed bones of each stump. But then his arm was free and he wheeled onto his side; the cleaver nicked his shoulder and sunk into the table again and he wrestled frantically with the second strap, pain howling up his arm. His ruptured stomach split and blood sprayed his torso, exploding from his wounded hand. He was sobbing, he realised, tears stinging his eyes, arm throbbing, index finger and thumb useless in his mad scramble to unfasten the second buckle—

Almost useless. The strap snapped open and he ripped himself from the table, spiralling to climb off.

His legs. Still attached. Above him, the cleaver came down hard and ploughed into the table so forcefully it shook. Charlie rolled off, hanging from the table by his ankles, and screamed as his shin snapped loudly. Yanking his whole body back, he tipped the table towards him, wrenching the cleaver with it and out of the mad butcher's hand. Still shrieking, he fumbled with his good hand to undo the remaining buckles.

One leg free, Charlie looked up to see the butcher bearing down on him, climbing over the upturned table like some pig-faced monster. The boar's skull it wore as a mask was spattered with blood—Charlie's blood—and through one huge, cracked eye-socket Charlie saw the wild, bloodshot and entirely human eyes of a killer.

'*Leave me alone!*' he yelled, yanking his leg free and rolling to one side as the beast in the butcher's apron grabbed the cleaver and swung at his gut.

He remembered before. Before waking up, before this room, before this *thing*—before any of it. The smoke and shadow of the battlefield, and death all around him.

Where the hell was he now?

He'd died, he realised. He'd died out there

and this was hell. But he didn't *remember* dying. He remembered scrambling out of the arc of a stabbing pike, remembered cowering behind the corpse of one of his brothers-in-arms as he reloaded the musket, fumbling for a good couple of minutes to slide the ball into the barrel and set the thing to fire—

And good god, he'd never fired that shot.

Charlie's eyes widened and he glanced down toward the end of the table. His gun lay on the floor where he'd kicked it. Still loaded with one shot, one chance—and by god, he was probably dead, but if not...

He grabbed for the gun and the cleaver slashed the back of his leg. He howled as a bright, searing pain ripped his lower half to shreds, and then he was on his back, the musket pointed up into the grinning boar's face, and he pressed his finger to the trigger.

Wait...

One shot. *One* chance.

Charlie roared with everything in his stomach and thrust the barrel of the musket forward, plunging it into the huge eye-socket of the beast. The bone around the socket splintered, thin cracks running up into the top of the skull, and the thing wearing the boar's face for a mask growled so loudly it echoed.

The butcher staggered back, thick strings of blood flying from the blade of the cleaver and streaking the apron red.

Charlie drew in a deep, hitched breath as the butcher reached up with a thick-fingered hand, gently pushing up at the edges of the mask. The tusks of the great boar's skull dripped with red as he pulled and tugged and twisted it off...

'Holy Mary, mother of God,' Charlie whispered.

The skull fell to the floor, cracked around one eye and painted and smeared red.

The butcher took a step forward, brandishing the cleaver. His face was a mess of exposed flesh and muscle, streaked with white and pink but raw and red and embedded with a crust of salt. He had been skinned. His eyeballs were huge and wild, sunk into a meaty face but alive and rolling and mad. He was grinning—well, he may as well have been—with his cheeks shredded, sinews holding them together. His teeth flashed sharp and vicious.

Charlie heard a yell from outside and glanced toward the bloody window. Through the smeared panes he saw movement outside and his eyes widened. Dozens of them, almost a hundred, approaching the house. Bloody silhouettes through the glass.

The butcher swung his cleaver forward with a deep, wet roar and Charlie yelped as the very corner of the blade glanced across his throat, nicking beads of blood from his skin.

One shot.

One chance.

'Fuck you!' Charlie yelled, and he jabbed the musket into the butcher's raw-ribbon face with one hand and squeezed the clunky trigger.

The room exploded with a loud *crack!* and the butcher reeled back, skull spraying the walls as shot ripped through him. He crumpled to his knees, his neck a ragged nest of torn muscle and tendon.

Still gripping the cleaver, the headless

body of the butcher swayed forward, back, then forward again and collapsed.

Silence.

Charlie finally let out his breath, dropping the gun and nursing his ruined knuckles.

No...

Not silence.

Blood pooled wetly around the butcher's body, and as Charlie listened he heard it clearly: the buzzing of flies. But they were nowhere to be seen. The sound came from beneath the headless corpse, from all around it. But no flies, not anywhere.

Charlie found himself staring into the huge, black eyes of the boar's skull as the buzzing became a loud, incessant hum. And then he saw movement, in the corner of his eye.

The blood, still pooling around the carcass. But more than that; not pooling, but *spreading*.

He watched as it oozed to the walls, filling the floor, running in wide, red rivers into every corner, thick and stinking and *red*...

And then it began to spread upwards. Swathes of crimson trickled wetly up the walls toward the ceiling, glistening and shimmering in the thick, red light, and all the while the buzzing grew louder and louder.

Four shapes formed on the walls, one on each. Four red, wet silhouettes, knotting out of the bloody trails and widening, spreading arms, rearing heads—

Four more of *him*.

'Oh, shit,' Charlie said, and he screamed as the four bloody silhouettes started to twist themselves out of the walls and into the room.

CHAPTER SEVENTEEN
LET THEM IN

'All right, so... we're safe,' Abram said, 'in this room—we appear, at least, to be—for now.'

'Sure about that, boss?' Michael said, anger flaring in his face. 'You led us in here. Into this house. Figured that would be pretty safe too, huh?'

Abram looked right at him, eyes narrow.

His burnt face was something out of a nightmare; Michael felt a twang of guilt as he imagined the pain coursing through the older man's body. And he hadn't mentioned it, hadn't complained, not once.

'Sorry,' Michael began, 'I—'

'No, you make a perfectly good point,' Abram said quietly. 'And to all of you, I apologise. I made a mistake, leading us in here. But I couldn't have known of the various hells awaiting us inside... and faced with what we were, out there—'

'We know,' Edith nodded. Blood had begun to seep through the bandage knotted around her shoulder. She shared a soft look with Michael and smiled sadly at him. 'It's okay, General.'

'But how do we know we're safe in here?' Michael said, glancing around again. 'Everything I've seen so far has told me to come here—'

'—me too,' Abram cut in.

'And me,' Edith whispered.

'So how do we know it's not just the worst trap of all?' Michael finished.

A moment's uneasy quiet. Then he turned his head to look in Morgan's direction. The young man had been silent throughout.

'What about you?' he said. 'How did you get here?'

Morgan opened his mouth to reply, but Abram cut in: 'It doesn't matter *how* we all got here, it only matters how we get out.'

'But... if we're safe here,' Edith said.

'We don't entirely know that we are,'

Michael shrugged.

'True,' Abram nodded. 'And even if we are, we can't stay here forever. Food and water, for one thing. For another...'

Michael became aware of something, then. A noise in the background, not in the library itself but slipping like a bandit through the walls; something that sounded like the muffled yells of an angry mob.

'It's safe,' Morgan said suddenly. 'It must be. Think about it. All along, *something* was leaving you notes. Some*one*, maybe. Leaving you clues, trying to get you to find this place. But the house wouldn't let you.'

'Until it did.'

'Yes—*all at once*. It didn't want you here, it wanted you separated, split up—dead—but then *something changed*. What?'

Michael swallowed. There was something about the way the wounded soldier was speaking, something that didn't feel right. 'I don't...'

'What changed?' Morgan said. 'What happened, in those last moments before the library opened up to you?'

There it was again. Michael frowned. For a moment it sat uneasily on his throat, pressing it closed, making it difficult to breathe—and then he realised what Morgan had been saying, what he had been saying *wrong*, what that could mean. 'What do you—'

'Oh, god, *you*,' Edith said.

Michael's brow furrowed. He turned to her. But she wasn't looking at him, or Morgan; her eyes were on Abram.

Abram shook his head. 'What?'

Edith looked at Michael, then at Abram again. 'What happened, in those last moments before we got here? What changed?'

'I don't...'

Outside, the muted yelling had grown louder. Closer.

Abram's eyes widened. 'I found myself in the living room,' he said. 'I crawled out of a fireplace and found myself in there, with you. And those things...'

'The family,' Morgan said.

'The family,' Edith nodded.

'And I said... Christ, it *was* me,' Abram said. 'I told you I'd seen them. Out of the window.

The soldiers Morgan warned us about, in the forest. Coming for the house.'

'And what else did you say?' Edith said. 'That there were more of them than we'd thought. That there must have been *seventy* of them.'

'At least.'

Michael looked toward the thick, red curtains halfway down the wall. Quickly, he moved to them, drew them open. The rail rattled loudly.

Out of the window, he saw what Abram had seen. 'Holy hell,' he murmured.

The Cavaliers had come out of the woods, bloody from battle. Lush uniforms and plumed headgear, torn and ragged, gave away their allegiance with the crown. They held flaming pikes and muskets, and they spread across the field between Price Manor and the forest, marching deliberately toward the house.

'It heard you,' Michael realised. 'The house heard you.'

Abram nodded. 'The house wants men. Wants bodies. Why bother with four—'

'—five—'

'—why bother with *five*, when it can have *dozens*?'

'So it wants us to lure them here,' Edith realised.

'Well, job done,' Michael shrugged. 'Does that mean it'll let us go?'

'Wait, you're not seriously considering *allowing* it to have them.'

He looked at her. 'We were going to have to kill them all anyway.'

'They were going to kill *us*,' Edith argued. 'We never had a chance.'

'No, but now we do. Now we have the upper hand,' Abram said quietly behind them. 'It would be easy. Far easier than it would have been. All we'd have to do would be to let them in... and the house would take care of the rest.'

Edith joined Michael at the window, looking down at the approaching Royalists. They seemed so far away, like insects beneath them, and yet in their numbers the force was undeniably terrifying. And they were getting closer every second.

'We have to do it,' Abram said. 'So we can get out of here. So we can complete our mission.'

'For Christ's sake, *fuck* your mission!' Edith yelled, slamming her hands on the sill. She winced as pain rocked her wounded shoulder.

'Your mission...' Michael whispered. He wheeled around suddenly, turning on Morgan again. 'A minute ago, you said *you*.'

'What?'

'You said the house "wanted *you* separated". That something was "leaving *you* notes". Not "we". Not "us". *You*, as in, the three of us.'

'What are you getting at, Shuck?' Abram said.

'He said, "What happened, in those last moments before the library opened up to you?"'

'And?'

'He didn't say, "What happened before the library opened up to *us*?"'

'Jesus, Michael, what's your fucking point?' Edith snapped.

Michael hesitated. He looked Morgan right in the eyes. 'My point is, how did *you* get here?'

Morgan appeared to swallow nervously.

'That's it?' Edith said suddenly. 'That's your point? Christ, Shuck, there are more important things going on here.'

'Getting out,' Abram nodded. 'The mission.'

'*Fuck* the god-damned mission!' Edith repeated. 'Christ, man, get some fucking perspective! We're in hell with all the demons and devils you could ever imagine, and you still want to kill one man?'

'Agreed,' Michael nodded. 'Fuck the mission.'

Edith looked at him, cocking an eyebrow. 'Really? You're with me, now?'

Michael shrugged. 'I just want to go home.'

Abram' eyes flared with fire, with the same fire that had burned his flesh so horribly, and he snapped. 'All that we've sacrificed in the name of this mission, and you're prepared to give up on it now?'

'What does it matter if he lives or dies?' Michael said quietly. 'You're not ridding the world of evil by ridding it of one man.'

'A decidedly evil man,' Abram argued.

'True, but... god, how many would we have to kill before the world was a better place, man? And by the time we got there, when we'd finally done them all... what would we be? Just as bad as them? Or worse?'

Abram paused.

'Who?' Morgan said suddenly.

Edith looked at him, as if remembering he was there.

'Who do you plan to kill?' Morgan said. 'Who is the mission?'

Abram looked grimly in Michael's direction. Michael nodded.

'Cromwell,' Abram said flatly.

Morgan frowned. 'I don't...'

'Cromwell gave us our orders, directly,' Abram said. 'He formed our little band—the Nowhere Boys—in the hopes that we could win this filthy *fucking* war for him. All around, there was nothing but Roundheads fighting Cavaliers, us against the enemy. Against the crown. He knew that that could go on for years—decades—without getting us anywhere.'

'So he had us do things,' Edith cut in. 'Dark and secret things. Things that would help us win. He had the Nowhere Boys go places others couldn't—'

'—do things others *wouldn't*—'

'—and all the while,' Michael said, 'he revealed himself to us. The man we're fighting for is just as much a devil as the men we're fighting.'

'He gave us one last mission,' Abram said. 'And I decided... no more. I wouldn't have my people, my brothers—my sister—do his bloodwork anymore. So I gave us a new mission.'

'To kill Cromwell,' Morgan said.

'Yes.'

Morgan paused for a moment, as if considering. Then he nodded. 'Okay.'

'Okay?'

'I've heard the stories,' he said, gazing out of the window. 'About him. The things he's done.'

'Either way,' Michael said, 'mission or no mission, we need to get out of this place.'

'Agreed,' Edith said.

'Agreed,' Abram nodded.

'And what about the kid?' Edith said. 'What about Charlie?'

'I'll find him,' Morgan said. 'I'll get him out of here.'

'No,' she said, 'we won't leave you here. We'll all—'

'I don't think we have a choice,' Michael said quietly. He looked at Morgan. 'Do we?'

Edith frowned. 'What?'

Morgan shook his head. 'No. No choice. I'll stay here and find the kid.'

'What?' Edith said, looking from one man to the other. 'What do you mean, no choice?'

'He has to stay,' Michael said.

Morgan nodded.

'What? Why?'

'Tell her—tell *us*—how you got here,' Michael said.

Morgan nodded again. 'I found myself in an attic. I ran, to get away from... well, something. And I found myself in an attic room. And she found me.'

'She?'

'An old woman. A spirit of some kind. She looked... half-dead, skeletal. She came for me...'

Gingerly, Morgan reached up and touched the back of his skull. He blinked.

'She was stronger than I thought she'd be. She pinned me to the wall, grabbed the back of my head, and then... I felt her fingers, digging in...'

'And then you were here,' Michael guessed. 'Very suddenly, I presume.'

Morgan nodded.

'No...' Edith said. 'She didn't...'

'I think she did, I'm afraid,' Abram said, leaning back to look at the back of Morgan's head.

Morgan turned, slowly, and Edith gasped.

His cranium was split open, a deep welt in the back of his skull the size of a handprint. Brain matter dribbled down the back of his neck, pink and glistening.

He turned again, and she saw that one of his eyes was rolled up in his head and clouded with a fine red mist. She hadn't noticed before.

'I died,' he said, 'and what dies in this house stays in this house.'

Michael swallowed, guilt pressing on the walls of his stomach.

'I can't ever leave,' Morgan said. 'But you can.'

CHAPTER EIGHTEEN
LET US OUT

Gingerly, Edith pushed open the library door. 'Sure about this, boss?' she said.

Beside her, Abram nodded. 'Only way out is *out*,' he said.

Michael laid a gentle hand on Edith's arm. 'You sure you're okay with it?'

She looked up at him and smiled sadly. 'It's like you said,' she whispered. 'Ether way, we were going to at least try to kill these people. That's war, Shuck. We knew what we signed up for.'

Michael swallowed. Nodded. 'Sure.'

Abram shook his head. 'There's enough of them. The four of us... the *three* of us survived this long. I'd imagine this lot stand a better chance still. I'd just rather not be around to see it.'

Michael cocked an eyebrow. 'You think they'll be all right?'

Sombrely, Abram shook his head. 'We've been fighting these people for years, Caldwell. Years that have felt like lifetimes. Truth be told... Christ save me, the *absolute* truth be told... I truly don't give a shit if they make it or not.

'That's the real cost of war, my friends. Not the wretched loss of life, not the devastation and blood, the loss and grief and sorrow left in its wake... no, the real cost is what it does to those who're left. I thought all this death would make me soft, would tear me apart, but... it's just made me cold. Hollow inside. And if letting a troop of men who were sent to kill us die means that we might escape that same fate, then I'm all for it.'

Edith opened her mouth. Closed it. 'We win, then,' she said eventually.

He looked at her and offered the same sad smile that she'd perfected. 'Some victories feel like falling.'

'Then this is where the Nowhere Boys fall,' Michael said. 'And after this...'

'Let's focus on now, shall we?' Edith said, glancing out onto the landing and flexing her fingers around the shaft of her pike. 'It's clear. I doubt this house will let us go so easily, but if we go now...'

'I wonder if this house will fall someday,' Michael said quietly. 'Even devils die, right?'

'I say it's already fallen,' Abram said gravely. 'There's no devil in Hell or on Earth that could kill so carelessly, so cruelly, without having reached its lowest point.'

Edith grimaced, opened the door wide, and led Michael and Abram out onto the landing.

Michael looked back through the open door as he stepped out. Morgan stood in the middle of the library, hands by his sides, leaning heavily on his crooked leg. Michael wondered briefly if he could still feel the pain.

He nodded. 'Good man,' he whispered, and the three of them headed down the landing toward the stairs. Michael's grip tightened on his knife as the door groaned on its hinges and slammed shut. When he looked back, it was gone.

The corridor was long and narrow, the blue

walls tainted by the feral amber lights of candles dripping steadily over brackets clamped to them at regular intervals. Edith could see the stairs ahead of them, leading down into the entrance hall. An easy path down, then. Nothing to—

She froze at the top of the stairs. The three of them could all hear it: the rattling and knocking of fists on wood. Slowly, Edith turned her head and looked down into the hallway.

The door bent and shuddered in its frame, the silhouettes of soldiers outside smeared over the glass panes of narrow windows either side.

'We're gonna have to find another way out,' Abram said. 'If we can get into the kitchen—'

'The window,' Edith nodded. Her eyes were still on the trembling front door. She heard yelling voices, the slow, deliberate thumps of something heavy against the wood. How had they not broken through already? 'But the kitchen... when I was there before, it was in ruins. I don't know if we can get back.'

'Then we find another window,' Michael said, looking down the landing. All the doors had disappeared save for one right at the end; a crude, splintered slab of wood with a window of crystalline glass in its centre, through which a sizzling white light flickered. 'Through there,' he suggested.

'Works for me,' Abram said.

Edith stood at the top of the stairs. The house around them was silent, passive; it wasn't trying to attack them anymore. She glanced back toward the door; it looked as though the place was even offering them a way out. All because they'd agreed to damn the lives of dozens of men. To feed the manor. All because they'd agreed to let it win.

'It's not right,' she whispered. 'They should have broken in by now.'

Downstairs, the dreadful thumping on the door continued.

'What?' Michael said.

'The house... it's giving us time to find another way out. It's *thanking* us.'

Neither of the men said anything.

'It's not right,' Edith echoed.

Michael looked to Abram, then back to her. 'Agreed,' he said. 'But if we try to warn them, try to turn them away...'

'They won't believe us,' Abram said. Bubbles of blistered skin trembled softly across his burned cheek. 'As far as they know, we're safe in here. Whatever you say to them, they'll try and get in.'

'And the house will try and kill us all over again,' Michael said.

Edith nodded. Paused. 'So—'

'Yes,' Abram said.

She looked back at him. 'Yes?'

He looked at Michael, then nodded at her. 'Do it. Warn them. Give them the best chance you can.'

Michael nodded his agreement. 'It's already tried to kill us once, right? We know there's a way out'—he gestured to the door at the end of the landing—'so we know there's a chance. However small it becomes.'

Whispering, outside the front door. Edith listened, but could not make out the words. The thumping had stopped.

'Okay,' she said, 'ready to run?'

The two men nodded. 'Always,' Michael said.

Edith stood at the railing, gripping the banister with both hands, and took a deep breath.

'You there!' she yelled. Her voice carried across the entrance hall and to the door, and she saw the shadows through the narrow windows freeze. She glanced in Michael's direction, her eyes wide and frightened. Uncertain.

He nodded.

'You there!' she called again. 'Listen to me!'

Something groaned in the walls. As if the house were waking up.

'Listen to me! Do not open that door! This house is not what you think it is! You wait out there, and we will—gladly—come out to you! Please, just don't come in! Don't open that door!'

'The house is evil!' Abram yelled, leaning over the banister. Behind him, a soft breeze carried down the landing. An exalted sigh. Or a sharp intake of breath. The house was preparing...

'It's possessed by some spirit, or demon!' Edith called. 'It is not safe in here! Turn back, turn away! Please!'

There was a moment of silence. Of consideration.

And then someone outside said, quietly, 'Fire.'

All at once the house exploded. The door crashed inwards at the unholy *crack!* of muskets firing. Shadows pushed toward the opening as thick, grey mist rolled into the entrance hall and burned with an unseen spray of candlelight.

A figure in elaborate uniform stepped slowly into the wreckage, brushing down his armour. He looked up toward the landing and smiled, teeth flashing in the smoke.

'Run!' Edith screamed, and then the house attacked.

Morgan heard the gunshots, but already they sounded distant, faded, as though the house had carried the library into some far corner of its being. He heard the door fall in, and it sounded as though the sound were travelling through thick soup.

And then he heard a bell ring. The scratching of a quill on paper.

He frowned.

A flood of soldiers crowded into the entrance hall, roaring with bloodlust. 'Up there!' one yelled, pointing up at the landing—and then a splintered spear of hard wood thrust up from the floor beneath him and plunged into the base of his chin, shooting out the top of his head and spraying the wall with blood.

Another of the soldiers screamed as groping, pale white hands clawed and scratched at him from the wall, from *within* it, as if they were made of the very fabric of the building itself. A third turned and fired blindly into the corner of the hallway; Edith looked and saw shadows boiling in the dark, jerking and twisting up into thin, clawed figures.

'Come on!' Michael yelled, grabbing her hand and yanking her away from the banister.

The three of them turned and bolted down the landing as the floor beneath them rippled, jagged splinters of wood shooting up at them. Dark shapes moved fluidly across the walls and Edith looked up to see that a long, jagged crack was following their movements along the ceiling, chunks of debris falling. She screamed as a loud *crack!* boomed through the corridor and a hunk of plaster the size of her head smacked the floor inches behind her.

She glanced back and saw Cavaliers coming up the stairs, roaring and raising muskets high—

'Down!' she yelled, shoving Michael's head down as one of the soldiers fired. The *bang!* was incredible and rang in her ears, the shot ripping chunks out of the wall. The door at the end of the landing was farther away, growing farther still with every second.

Edith heard more screaming downstairs and the sick, wet *crunch* of bones breaking. The spatter of blood on hardwood floors, the groaning and screaming of the walls coming in to crush whoever was left down there.

'God damn it!' Abram yelled as a hand of

knotted, red-veined wood bent up from the floor and grabbed at his ankle. He stamped it down and tumbled forward, reaching the door and yanking it open. 'In!'

Edith shoved Michael through the door and followed quickly, slamming it behind her. The flickering white light of the room was blinding and she squinted, whirling around as, out on the landing, a Cavalier soldier shrieked in agony. The visceral *splutch* of something ripping open was followed by the soft patter of blood on the door.

'Bathroom,' Michael breathed, looking around. 'Wonder if Morgan ever found—'

The room started to shift. Edith looked up, panting heavily, the pike shaking in her hands, to see the squarish bathroom start to stretch, to elongate.

'The window!' she said, pointing across the room. At the far end—getting farther from them with every moment—a tall, wide window made of the same frosted glass that formed a pane in the bathroom door. 'Quick, before—'

The bathroom tipped to one side and the

tiles started to splinter.

'Run!' Edith yelled, and they tumbled forward into the chaos.

Morgan pressed his ear to the library door, heard soldiers screaming as they thundered past. He was somewhere downstairs, he realised; he could hear them flooding in through the front door, one by one, screaming as the entrance hall attacked them.

Behind him, an unseen bell rang steadily. *Ding! Ding! Ding!*

He waited for it to stop, for the awful scratching that accompanied it to stop, and then he pressed gently on the door and pushed it open.

The entrance hall was a mess of blood and bodies and he was reminded of the battlefield outside—but these were not his men, not his brothers. Still, they had never deserved to die like this...

Balking, Morgan passed quietly through the carnage and headed for the kitchen.

The bathroom was still stretching and expanding, becoming a long tunnel of tiled walls and mirrored surfaces. With every yard they ran the house seemed to yank the far wall back another ten feet.

'We'll never make it!' Edith yelled, her eyes frantically scouring the walls. Shadowy shapes rippled across the tiles, hands reaching and clawing. She leapt over a rusted copper pipe that bent and swerved across the floor and turned her head, staring at the door they'd come through. A shape appeared in the glass, reached for the handle—and something yanked it back and out of view. She heard the Cavalier scream. 'God, it's killing them all!'

'Keep running!' Michael grunted, thrusting the blade of his knife into a slick, wet mouth that had opened up in the wall beside him. Claws and hands and stretching, yawning maws filled with teeth opened up between the tiles, pushing out from the grouting and the gaps, cracking loudly—

There was a roar and a great splash as a porcelain toilet bowl erupted outward and a huge, long creature thrashed out of it. Edith's eyes widened as the lizard-like thing slithered out of the bowl and snapped at Abram's legs. 'Catch!' she yelled, tossing her pike toward him.

Abram glanced up, reaching out and fumbling to catch the spear. He swung—

The shaft of the pike crashed into the creature's throat and splintered, splitting in two. The brown-skinned thing roared again, its belly rumbling, spines and rivets of leathery armour rippling across its back. Abram staggered back, thrusting one of the broken halves of the pike up and into the thing's soft-skinned chin—

The reptile screamed and scuttled back, slamming its tail into Abram's shin as it swept past him. 'Keep running!' Edith yelled, grabbing his arm as she passed.

Behind her, Michael turned to look back at the door. 'It's opening!' he screamed.

'Then we have to *go*,' she yelled back.

Edith yelped as she passed by a long, gold-framed mirror on her left and a dark shape flitted across the glass, just behind her reflection, right on her tail. A moment later she passed by another mirror on her right and saw the shadowy creature above her, raking its claws down toward her head—

She caught sight of a movement in a third mirror, on her left, before she passed it—and ducked as a glass-skinned beast crashed out of the surface, screaming with a splintered throat as it swiped at her. Its teeth were jagged shards of glass in a face that was made up of them, and Edith crumpled to the floor beneath its swinging arms, sliding on her knees and rolling onto her back in time to see Michael slam his whole body into the glass thing and shatter it into pieces, screaming as fragments tore and shredded his skin and his face.

'Down!' Abrams yelled, grabbing Michael and shoving him to the floor, throwing himself down onto the tiles a moment later. Edith's eyes widened as a huge, brown shape flew through the air behind them—

And the monster crashed into the window and fell, crashing and screeching, through it.

Glass sprayed the bathroom and Edith

yelled in agony as rough-edged splinters gouged deep welts in her cheeks and neck. Covering her face, she looked up to see the door at the far end of the room and opened wide, watched in horror as Cavalier soldiers poured through—

'Go,' Abram said, hauling her up onto her feet. 'Now.'

She looked at Michael, then to the window. Glancing through the shattered frame she saw the reptilian beast laying on wet, dewy grass outside, sprawled on its back and broken. Michael nodded.

Edith looked past Abram, to the soldiers crashing into the bathroom. Watched as the tiles started to explode and shatter around them.

And then she grabbed Michael's hand, nodded, and the two of them climbed up and leapt awkwardly out of the window, screaming all the way down.

CHAPTER NINETEEN
CHARLIE

The kitchen door was—almost surprisingly—exactly where it had been before, except now Morgan had to step over a dozen smouldering carcasses to reach it. He could hear the carnage upstairs: the shattering of glass, and the ever-present rise and fall of screaming. Down here, though, the manor was a wasteland of post-chaotic death; a graveyard where the only dignity afforded to each body was a thick blanket of rolling fog coming through the front door.

As soon as Morgan passed through the kitchen door, the sounds from above fell into silence. He could hear nothing but his own pounding heart—and even that, he felt, must be in his imagination, a phantom echo, for he was certain his heart had ceased beating a while ago now.

'Hello?' he called.

The pink-blue tiles had shifted and changed, some cracked and splintered, and the table upon which they'd restrained the young man was gone.

Around the room, twelve doors—each one identical to the last, each one marked *Food Store*—surrounded him. Mocking him.

'Charlie?' he called, stepping into the middle of the room. A thin layer of chalk-white dust coated everything and made the air in the room toxic; it stung to breathe. He could smell blood.

He heard the buzzing of flies.

'Charlie...'

He froze as a muffled scream echoed behind one of the doors on his right. The pounding in his ears wasn't the sound of his heart beating, he realised, but the muted *thump-thump-thump* of something struggling.

'Charlie!'

Morgan careened toward the door and grabbed the handle. He slammed his fist on the wood and yelled again.

'Charlie, is that you?'

There was a grunt behind the door and another cry of pain. Morgan twisted the handle and shoved.

The door burst open and he fell through—not into the food store but into another kitchen, another version of the same kitchen, only this one was smeared wall-to-wall with blood. The window dripped with it, turning the light coming in to a kaleidoscope of brilliant red; the walls were covered, except for four distinct silhouettes where something had peeled the blood away, something in the shape of a man...

Charles Buxton sat with his back against the kitchen counter, his head lolling to one side. He was bruised, broken; missing fingers. His eyes lifted, only slightly, and widened at the sight of Morgan. There was something there, something like recognition, and Morgan hesitated. The kid had been passed out when they'd found him; Charles Buxton had never seen his face before. Or...

Morgan yelled as a cleaver swung at him. The blade sunk deep into his chest and his mouth opened; there was no pain. He looked down, saw the cleaver jammed into his ribs, but there was no blood either.

No blood pumping through his body anymore.

The butcher stared at him, a huge man with a face of exposed, salted muscle, and for a moment there was surprise. Then Morgan wrenched the blade from his chest and kicked out, landing his boot in the giant's belly and sending him stumbling back.

'Charlie, let's—'

Morgan blinked. Across the room, another man—a butcher, same as the first, wearing the same blood-smeared apron, his face skinned just the same—was coming for Charlie with his cleaver raised high.

Movement behind him, and Morgan whirled around to see a third coming for him. The same man, the same monster. He remembered what the ghoulish woman in the attic had said:

The butcher. He came here once...

Morgan ducked as another cleaver swung for his head, missing him by inches and *whoosh*ing through the air. The blade buried itself in the wall and he turned his head, saw a fourth blood-soaked copy of the monstrous butcher brandishing a fourth gleaming cleaver.

Those who die here, stay here.

Across the room, Charlie moaned with agony as the butcher standing over him lashed out with a thick, knotted fist and cracked his nose open. Blood poured down his face in a greasy, red wall.

What killed him? he had asked.

'Jesus!' Morgan yelled as two ghastly figures rounded on him, backing him up against the door he'd come in through. The butcher was horrific, a mess of meaty flesh and bunched muscles, and he was grinning. Enjoying this. Loving it.

All four of him.

The family, she'd said. *My family...*

Morgan backed up, eyes flitting between Charlie and the pair of butchers pressing him against the wall. He fumbled for the handle, twisting his body to one side as the first flung its cleaver toward his ribs. It sunk into the wood.

The room directly behind him should have been the kitchen. The other kitchen. But this house had its own rules.

'Please,' he whispered. 'Please, we brought you all this food... just let me have this.'

And he yanked the door open and sunk to his knees.

For a moment, there was nothing. Morgan looked up; the butcher loomed over him, raised the cleaver high—

And a wet, black tentacle whipped over Morgan's head and coiled around the butcher's neck, squeezing so hard that something popped.

Morgan rolled out of the way as they came through the door behind him: a young girl first, her entire body exploding with ink-black tentacles that thrashed madly into the room and for the throats of the butchers. The rest of the family followed: Father, his eyes the same ink-black, his hands spread and fingers curled into claws; Mother, her mouth open in a devastating scream; a young boy who Morgan could only assume was the girl's brother, his body stitched into strange and ungodly shapes.

Morgan's eyes snapped open wide as Father twisted his hands in opposite directions; the other side of the room, one of the four hulking butchers wailed in agony as his skin flayed itself open and blood pooled down his body in thick rivers. Mother stepped forward, cracking her neck back and moaning through her wide-open mouth. A second butcher sunk to his knees in response, clamping both hands over his eardrums—exposed and smooth against the sides of his head—as they burst wetly. The stitched-up dog-boy lunged for the throat of the nearest butcher and all the while the girl stood in the middle of it all, shooting tentacles out of her body that attached themselves like long, wild leeches to the faces and necks of the monstrous, aproned beasts.

'Charlie! Now!' Morgan yelled, scrambling forward and grabbing the young man's good arm. He yanked him onto his feet and they staggered back toward the open door.

The butchers' kitchen erupted in a shower of blood as the family tore into them, ripped them apart. Morgan glanced back; the door had slammed closed, and he wrestled with the handle again, hauled it open.

Steam poured out of the room beyond as an unbearable wave of heat throbbed into the kitchen. Morgan saw machinery through the open door, watched the searing glow of firelight rise up the riveted shells of furnaces and thick, copper pipes. This room was new.

'Fuck it,' he murmured, grabbing Charlie and throwing the kid through the door. He followed, taking one last look into the kitchen before slamming the door behind them.

'What the hell is going on?' Charlie breathed, crumpling to his knees.

Morgan stood beside him on a dais made of rusted metal meshwork, looking around at the machines that filled the room. They were unfamiliar, strange—ripped straight from some loud, boiling future—and yet they looked simultaneously ancient, rusted and broken and battered as though they had been in use for years. Heat rolled off the open grille of a metal-walled furnace; boilers lined one wall like huge, white-hot barrels, each one decorated with a dial that practically trembled with pressure. A metal walkway screamed through the guts of the boiler room and beneath them, the floor was a pit of charcoal and fire. The heat was impossible.

'You saved me,' Charlie whispered. 'From that... man. That thing.'

'Not yet,' Morgan said quietly. 'I have to get you out of this place.'

'Where are we?'

'Right deep inside the devil's throat,' Morgan murmured, gazing around almost absent-mindedly. 'I think it's still trying to swallow us.'

He heard running footsteps upstairs. Another scream.

'All those men...' Charlie whispered.

'Cavalier men,' Morgan reminded him.

And then he paused. Frowned.

Turned.

'What is it?' Charlie said, standing awkwardly on his feet. His whole body twisted up with pain. 'What's wrong?'

'You weren't with us,' Morgan said. 'When we saw the Cavalier forces advancing, when we let them in... you were somewhere else.'

'I... saw them, through the window,' Charlie frowned. 'What are you—'

'And I know you, don't I? It's been bugging me, but... I've seen your face before. Just for a moment. I've...'

And then he remembered.

CHAPTER TWENTY
BEFORE (REVISITED)

Morgan roared over the sounds of musket fire and pounding blood in his ears, rage crashing through him as he fought his way uphill. Smoke poured down from the top of the mound and tried desperately to claw at him, to pull him onto his stomach, and with gritted teeth he fought against it, lashing out with his pike as soldiers screamed past him.

A musket barrel rose up into his face and he ducked, swinging an arm up to wrestle the gun from its wielder's hand. Screaming, he rammed the pike forward and into the Cavalier's armpit; their grip loosened and he grabbed the gun, swinging it round—

He fired as a young Cavalier soldier raged towards him. The musket bucked with a loud *crack!* in his hands. Shot smacked the young soldier's gut and the man shrieked as his stomach opened up beneath his uniform. Blood sprayed the smoke and Morgan ploughed forward, leaving the Cavalier to drop to the ground, clutching his belly.

'Roundhead scum!' someone yelled, right in Morgan's ear, and then there was a sharp pain in his leg as a serrated knife plunged into his calf. He screamed, tumbling down the hill in an explosion of smoke and blood as his leg gave way.

The last thing he saw before he passed out—brief as his sleep would be—was the sky. Beautiful, blood-red and raining down on them all.

Charles Buxton collapsed, clamping both hands over the mesh of bloody welts across his stomach. Fog all around him made it impossible to see. He moaned, dropping onto his face in the mud. The Cavaliers were fleeing, he realised, drawing back across the hill and towards the woods.

They were losing. Somehow, his battalion

was losing.

Everyone else was dead. Everyone. Dead or dying, at least—he heard screams grinding through the smoke and gasped as pain rocked his whole body.

Charlie tried to run, to stand, but it was no good. With every movement his stomach threatened to rip itself all the way open. He opened his mouth to scream for help but his men were gone, they were all gone—

But no. The Roundheads had won this battle. Somebody here would be kind. Would help him. If he could just...

Charlie scrambled desperately with the bloody earth, crawling for the nearest carcass. He moaned with pain as he fumbled for the corpse's rounded, metal helmet.

Pulling the Roundhead's uniform on over his own, grunting as agony made every movement unbearable, Charlie transformed himself. Gritting his teeth against the pain, he lifted the helmet onto his head—

And a musket ball smacked the back of the helmet, pain drilling into his skull and ringing in his ears and the helmet quaked against his skull and something cracked and there was pain, so much pain, and then—

His body convulsed as something in his brain exploded, and then shadows consumed him and he was asleep.

CHAPTER TWENTY-ONE
NOWHERE FALLS

For a moment, Edith was flying. Shards of glass rained down with her as she lurched through the air, a wave of air pushing at her body, ripping at her skin as she plummeted—

The ground caught her.

Edith gasped as the wind was knocked out of her stomach. Something broke with a loud, sickening *snap* and she clutched her leg, rolling onto her back. Beside her, Michael scrambled at the earth, trying to right himself. Behind them both, the corpse of the lizard-monster twitched and jerked as its last, frantic breaths shuddered from a heaving stomach.

Edith looked up. 'Abram!' she yelled. 'Get out of there!'

Silence. Her heart leapt into her mouth as

she stared up the dark wall of the manor, waiting for a shape to appear in the window, for the general to—

The thunderous *crack!* of a musket blast echoed all around them and Abram was blown backwards out of the window.

Edith yelled as he fell, blood streaking from his chest in ribbons as his head tipped back. He seemed to fall for a lifetime, scraps of skin that had clung to his burned face ripped off in the wind that his flailing body struggled with, and then he had landed.

Edith looked to Michael, and then—twisting her body—to the fallen general.

He was still.

'No,' she whispered, crawling toward him, her whole body on fire. 'No...'

'Edith, look out!' Michael yelled.

She whipped back her head, staring up at the shattered window. A Cavalier soldier stood in the frame, aiming his musket barrel down at them. His face was hysterical, his teeth flashing in a terrible grimace. 'Die, you treasonous bastards!' he screamed, bracing his hands on the gun to fire.

And then the window closed up. shards of glass knitted together, reforming so fast that it was like a wall of water spreading into the middle of the frame. Edith heard a scream behind the glass, saw blood spray it from outside, and then the soldier's left arm and a part of his right hand fell through the air, still gripping the musket.

The severed limbs hit the ground with a wet *thump*, and Edith began to breathe again.

Something cracked loudly as Morgan threw his knuckles into Charlie's face. He felt the soft bones of the young man's nose sink into his skull and heard the screaming, but all he saw was red. Steam rose and plumed around them and anger flooded his chest and he punched the boy again.

Again.

Again.

'You're one of them!' he yelled. 'You bastard, you were one of them all along!'

Charlie's eyes rolled back in his head, his face ruined and bloody. He grinned. 'Not just one of them,' he rasped. 'I watched your men surveying that field. I knew you'd be... easy pickings. I *led* them to you. My whole battalion. Dozens of men. And you...'

'And we sent you running into the woods,' Morgan spat, slamming Charlie's back against the smouldering hot shell of a boiler with a *clang*. 'Worked out well for you, huh?'

'Not running,' Charlie hissed. 'Regrouping. That was always the plan. Exhaust you on that hill, retreat and let you and your men scatter, and then pick you off. One by one.'

Morgan snarled. 'Well, looks like that didn't work out too well either.'

Charlie shook his head, grimacing as heat seared his back. 'Forgive me for not accounting for a demon house.'

'Forgiven,' Morgan said, and he grabbed Charlie by the ears and slammed his head into the boiler.

Charlie howled, sinking to his knees. All around them the room seemed to fume with pressure, heat rising in shimmering clouds and rolling across the ceiling. The boiler shuddered.

Morgan stepped back, rolling up his sleeves.

'So you're not going to get me out of here?' Charlie said.

'All my men died,' Morgan said flatly. 'Friends. Brothers. And for what?'

'For the *king*.'

'For nothing,' Morgan growled. 'And all because you led them to us. And now you're... smiling about it?'

Charlie laughed, blood streaming from his nose. Behind him, a blossom of red-tinged smoke rose from the base of the boiler. 'I don't care if I die here,' he said. 'All I wanted was to kill some *fucking* Roundheads—and I managed that, didn't I?'

Morgan shrugged. 'Fine,' he said, and he lunged forward and punched the young man in the throat.

Charlie gasped. 'So... you're going to—let us both... die in here?'

Morgan flexed his bloody knuckles and smiled again. 'Nope,' he said, 'just you.'

'But you can't—'

'Can't what?' Morgan said. 'Get out? No,

that's for damn sure. I'm stuck here forever. And when I've killed you, you worthless pig-fucker, you will be too. And then you're mine. And if we've got to spend forever in this house, you and me... oh, just think of all the ways I can find to hurt you.'

Charlie swallowed. Smoke rose up around them and the grille of a furnace behind Morgan trembled as a wave of heat erupted from it.

The house was laughing.

The field echoed with the sounds of slamming doors as the house closed up, sealing the Cavalier soldiers inside. Edith heard screaming, yelling, crying, gunshots and shattering brickwork, and she drew in ragged breaths, sobbing over Abram's bloody chest.

'Seventy men,' Michael murmured. 'Jesus Christ...'

They were the sounds of battle. Shrieking, crying, shooting, dying. And there was nothing they could do. A whole army inside that house, and they were losing.

'No,' Edith moaned, cradling Abram's blistered skull in her hands. 'No, you can't die, you can't... we have a mission to finish, remember?'

Abram moaned. His voice was throaty and terrible. 'No...' he rasped. Bubbles of blood rippled and burst across his chest. 'Don't go after... Cromwell. For all that man's done... he was never worth any of this. None of it.'

And then his eyes rolled up in his head and his chest was still.

Edith moaned, blood streaming down through her fingers. She looked desperately at Michael, and he laid a hand on her shoulder, shaking his head.

And there was nothing they could do.

'I thought... just for a moment, there... I thought there might be some way of winning. Some way of beating that house.'

'We got out,' Michael said softly. 'That's a win.'

Edith looked at him. 'Two of us,' she sobbed. 'We were the Nowhere Boys, Michael. And now... I knew we'd fall, eventually. But not today. Not here. I thought we'd *win*.'

Edith's body jolted as the crash of the slamming front door filled the air. She looked back, tears streaming down her face. 'Michael, look...'

The house was fading. A brilliant, white light burst through the windows, screaming through cracks between the stones of the walls, and smoke seemed to roll inwards at the feet of the building and clamber desperately up the towering fortress of death and blood—

And then it was gone, leaving only gun-smoke and burnt grass.

Michael blinked.

'As quickly as it came to be...' Edith murmured. 'Where do you think it went?'

Michael shook his head. 'I don't know. Back into Hell, I hope.'

Edith looked down at the dead man in her hands and choked back another sob. '*Back* into Hell?' she said. 'What about us, then, Shuck? Where are we?'

Michael laid his arm around her and kissed her forehead. 'Somewhere better than that place,' he said. 'At least it can't be any worse.'

The two of them looked out across the battlefield, and watched as the fog begin to clear and bright red bands of blood seeped through the soil.

ACKNOWLEDGEMENTS

Thanks, firstly, to everyone who's read this book. I can only hope that you enjoyed it at least half as much as the first two instalments of this series, of which I'm truly proud to be a part. And if you didn't, then don't give up on *Price Manor*; there are some truly excellent authors stepping in for the next few books, and I can't wait to see them on shelves. If you haven't read the first two yet—Mike Salt's *The House That Burns* and Jamie Stewart's *The House That Bleeds*—then check those out; they're really something.

Thank you to my Spooky Friends for letting me be a part of this. It's been an absolute privilege to write for this series and a lot of fun drawing the covers so far. Even if I'm not asked back for a future instalment, you can count on seeing more of those covers. With or without this series, though, the group of people that came together to put it together are some of the most supportive, terrifying and kind people I know.

Thanks to the history buffs that'll appreciate the amount of effort it took not to pepper this book with too many anachronisms (do you know how hard it is to say "typewriter" without saying "typewriter"?), and to those who'll let the odd one go like I did.

Thanks to my partner, as always, for everything and everything else.

ABOUT THE AUTHOR
JAY ALEXANDER

Jay Alexander is a lasagne-loving horror author from Norfolk, England. He writes slowly, gives up quickly, and struggles. Daily.

Jay's first folk horror collection, *Starving Grounds*, is coming in June 2022, and in the meantime you can find his work in anthologies from Snow-Capped Press, Black Hare Press, and DarkLit Press. For a taste of his folk horror work, check out "Black Dogs in the Dark" in the first edition of *Myth and Lore Zine*.

Jay also runs charity publishing house Dead Sea Press, and will be releasing aquatic horror anthologies through them until he (probably) dies. The first of these, *Terror in the Trench* and *Shadows on the Surface*, are available now on Amazon and all profits go to The Shark Trust. AVAILABLE NOW

THE HOUSE THAT BURNS
BOOK ONE IN THE **PRICE MANOR** SERIES

FROM **MIKE SALT,** AUTHOR OF **THE VALLEY** AND **THE HOUSE ON HARLAN.**

AVAILABLE NOW

THE HOUSE THAT BLEEDS
BOOK TWO IN THE **PRICE MANOR** SERIES

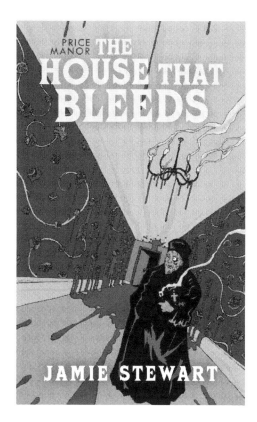

FROM **JAMIE STEWART,** AUTHOR OF **I HEAR THE CLATTERING OF THE KEYS (AND OTHER FEVER DREAMS).**

WANT MORE?

PRICE MANOR WILL RETURN...

Printed in Great Britain
by Amazon